Tales From the Liminal

STUDY EDITION

Tales From the Liminal
STUDY EDITION

S. K. Kruse

DEUXMERS

Published by Deuxmers, LLC
PO Box 437305, Kamuela, HI 96743
deuxmers.com

All stories originally published in *Tales From the Liminal*, 2021.
"The Stretch Motel" originally published in *Reed Magazine*, Issue 153 (2020).

Printed in the United States of America.
ISBN: 978-1-944521-36-3 (Softcover)
ISBN: 978-1-944521-24-0 (Ebook)
First edition, April 2025

CONTENTS

FOREWORD
by Dr. Timothy Carson

I have now taught ten semesters of liminal courses and seminars with college undergraduates. At the close of those classes I often ask them to engage in some kind of self-reflection. "What have you discovered? How do you see things differently now?" Two responses surfaced without fail.

The first is one of relief. Mostly relief that they are not crazy. Just knowing what liminality is and how it works is comforting, because it is a universal phenomenon, and everyone passes through those in-between spaces at one time or another. The old is gone but the new has not arrived yet. Identity is in flux. The way forward is uncertain but full of possibility. It's good to know that such transitions are normal. It is a relief.

The second is one of confidence. The reasoning goes this way: "Since I know what liminality is, now I can expect it and, most importantly, navigate its dark waters. I feel confident that I can be aware of what is happening when it is happening and make the passage. Not easily, but confidently.

I once had a student who climbed Mt. Kilimanjaro with her father and sister. They trained and prepared for it. The climb required strength, pacing, smarts, and endurance. Sometimes she felt like giving up. But they pushed on through this most liminal space outside the structure of their ordinary lives. They did achieve the summit. And then they descended back into the world of daily life, a life that was at once the same and different.

I asked her two questions. First, what did you leave behind on mount liminality? Second, what did you discover and bring forward with you? She thought for a moment and said, "What I left behind was years of self-doubt. What I discovered was the confidence that I could face anything. Afterall, I climbed Mt. Kilimanjaro."

My hope for those who dare to climb *Tales from the Liminal* is that they ascend the mystery of liminality in such a way that some things are left behind and other things are discovered. The path unfolds story by story, character by character. If this imaginative world of S.K. Kruse creates more perplexity than certainty, literary sojourners should know that they have arrived in the right place. I know that happened for my students as we read, studied, and discussed this most delightful book.

Timothy Carson teaches liminal studies in the Honors College of the University of Missouri, curates The Liminality Project, and is the author and editor of numerous books on liminality.

THE LIMINAL is a place, time, or state of being that's betwixt and between. Neither here nor there. If it's a place, it might be a staircase, airport, or refugee camp. If it's a time, it might be a summer of travel, a year of illness, or a period of war. If it's a state of being, it might be the experience of not fitting into the world's tidy categories and feeling like you exist somewhere between them. Or it might be the experience of no longer fitting into your *own* tidy categories but being unable to find a way out of them yet. If this is the case, you didn't end up there by accident. Something new is emerging in you, and for that to happen, some old things need to fall away. Darkness, confusion, and disorientation are to be expected. Just make sure you let the liminal do its work in you. You'll be glad you did.

For a more in-depth look at the liminal, please read Dr. Timothy Carson's introduction in the following pages.

AN INTRODUCTION TO THE LIMINAL

At the turn of the 20th century, anthropologist Arnold van Gennep identified broad patterns of renewal within indigenous, agrarian, pre-industrial communities. From his observations of the cultural rites and rituals that were utilized to foster those transitions, he came to understand a particular kind of social transition he named *The Rites of Passage*. That now well-known phrase became the title of a book by the same name that was published in 1909.[1] These rites not only fostered transition but protected the social group from the danger inherent in potential chaos during such transition. These rites accompanied almost every conceivable passage of life, including birth, matrimony, and death. Further, they honored the changing seasons of nature and marked disasters that afflicted individuals and communities.

The time and space when transitioning through a critical threshold is referred to as "liminality," based on the Latin root *limen*, which itself means threshold. In terms of rituals marking rites of passage, the movement includes a preliminal phase, the liminal middle, and reaggregation into a post-liminal reality. This pattern is demonstrated universally in different forms, practiced in many cultures. By the mid-20th century, anthropologist Victor Turner built upon and expanded van Gennep's work. As he defined society in terms of a structure of positions, his model of rites of passage became one of structure, antistructure, and re-structure.[2]

A person or group moving through the rites of passage became a liminal being, a passage person, and was ritually defined by special names, symbols, practices, and dress. They were typically ushered through the process by tribal elders who act as liminal guides. The cohort of initiates formed a special community around their shared liminality, a status Turner coined *communitas*.

Because liminal persons were passing from one known and definable status through an entirely uncertain one, they could represent social danger to the community. Those who were temporarily outside the structure of tribe and community become ritually unclean, a social definition known today when people live outside social norms and expectations.[3]

Transformation through this passage was understood to have resulted in a changed identity of the initiates; they have passed through symbolic death and rebirth into new ways of being and new status.[4] The locale of the passage itself was a highly symbolized locale of sacred time and space.[5] Though the great transitions have taken place in chronological time, they are also grounded in an idealized timelessness, a time beyond time.

Though it is common for an individual or community to pass from one state of being to another, there are also instances in which the state of liminality becomes ongoing or unending. Some semi-permanent forms of liminality are voluntary; people choose to enter the margins of society and live in alternative communities. But other forms of permanent liminality are involuntary, such as one finds in the aftermath of genocides, life-long incarceration, or living in the social margins of society as an outcast.

As an individual makes a critical transition, what is experienced in exterior rites and rituals is matched by a parallel interior movement. The liminal person departs from one definition of the self and transitions to a new level of consciousness. The symbolic mythic passage is internalized. One becomes a new being. In the contemporary world, these liminal realities take on many and varied forms. They arise through preestablished traditions or from a spontaneous response to events. They may or may not employ the guidance of identified liminal guides. The presence of community may or may not assist in the passage. And some forms of liminality may not include a sense of passage at all. In addition to an unfolding liminal passage that includes beginning, middle, and end, other forms of liminality are not so linear. Some in-between persons exist in the margins, on the edges of society, a place one enters voluntarily or without volition. Other liminal states exist in the intersections, in the space where one reality collides with another, creating an undefined third space that can be the source of either great confusion or creative genius. In our present culture, liminality is often experienced at the edge of any predictable or recognizable social landscape: abandoned cities, empty buildings, ruins, VR alternative reality, and the dystopian futurescapes of fictional literature or film. The consulting room of the therapist can serve as a modern equivalent to a rite of passage. Movie theaters provide an artificially created liminal time and space, as do adventure pilgrimages of many shapes and sizes.

Our present historical moment includes vast social conflict and dislocation, war and the aftermath of war, the rising specter of an ecological crisis, the impacts of pandemic, and an unknown technological future. Though people of all eras have known liminal phenomena, the people of our time have witnessed an exponential growth of liminality, in large part the result of rapid and complex change. We are living in a liminal moment of outsized proportion and intensity. And the many forms of liminality overlap and occur simultaneously.

An outline of the liminal process includes, in the broadest sense, an arc of passage, a loop as it were, that includes identifiable landmarks.[6] This arc is found in the great epic stories and narratives of world literature. Its aspects are recognizable in the content of dreams, the shape of mythic tales, and the plot of film. And it is known, most of all and most often, in the actual life experiences of people trying to make sense of them.

The arc of liminality includes crossing dramatic thresholds, leaving behind the old, descending into the darkness of the unknown, wandering in the wilderness, living with ambiguity and uncertainty, discovering new sign markers for the future, and transforming by way of a metaphorical rebirth. We also learn a new language with which we can name our many voluntary and involuntary transitions.

Arnold van Gennep, *The Rites of Passage* (London: Routledge and Kegan Paul, 1960).

Victor Turner, *The Ritual Process: Structure and Anti-Structure* (Chicago: University of Chicago Press, 1966).

Mary Douglas, *Purity and Danger* (New York: Frederick A. Praeger, 1966).

Emile Durkheim, *The Elementary Forms of the Religious Life* (New York: The Free Press, 1915).

Mircea Eliade, *The Sacred and the Profane* (New York: Harcourt Brace Jovanovich, 1959), 191.

Otto C. Scharmer, *The Essentials of Theoury U: Core Principles and Applications* (Oakland, CA: Berrett-Koehler Publishers, Inc., 2008), 103-106.

This excerpt is from *Leaning into the Liminal: A Guide for Counselors and Companions* (2024) by Timothy Carson and is used with permission of the publisher, The Liminality Press.

LIMINAL REFLECTION AND WRITING PROMPTS

CAN BE USED WITH ANY OF THE STORIES

- What are the liminal aspects of the story? What makes them liminal and what role do they play in the story?
- What challenges does the protagonist face in the liminal? How do they respond to these challenges?
- Is there a guide present to help the protagonist find their way through the liminal? If so, how do they help?
- Does the protagonist make it through the liminal? What did it take? Are there consequences for remaining in the liminal? How does the protagonist change after moving through the liminal to the other side?
- What are the liminal aspects of the story? How do they make you feel? Why do they make you feel this way?
- Have you had a liminal experience? What were the similarities and differences between your experience and that of the protagonist in the story?
- If you've had a liminal experience, did you have a guide to help you through? How did they help? What were the similarities and differences between your guide and the guide in the story?
- Do you think the protagonist of the story made good choices? Why or why not?
- Compare and contrast the liminal aspects of the story with another story.

Find out more about the
Tales From the Liminal Study Edition
and liminal writing opportunities.

CONTENT WARNINGS

Spoilers aren't any fun, but before you're swept away into the liminal, you might want to know what sort of content you'll be seeing:

Bigfoot's Got a Lover ▹ *A little profanity*

The Birthday Party ▹ *Death*

The Stretch Motel ▹ *Profanity (some real humdingers) and references to death*

Mistakes May Have Been Made ▹ *A little profanity, references to death, affairs, and nuclear holocaust*

All He Could Do Is Sing ▹ *Death*

When They Come For Me ▹ *Graphic violence, profanity (some real humdingers)*

The Ferryman and His Brother ▹ *References to death*

She Saw Gertrude Stein in the Condensation on Her Window ▹ *Profanity and an implied sexual encounter*

Goodbye, Bonavento ▹ *References to death and animal cruelty*

I Followed Schrodinger's Cat and Here's What I Found ▹ *No disclaimers*

The Unexpected Consequence of an Unsolicited Revolution ▹ *References to death*

Summoned by a Star ▹ *No disclaimers*

PRE-READING QUESTIONS

- Have you ever been kicked out of a group? How did that experience affect you?
- Have you ever altered your behavior or personality to fit in or be liked? What was the outcome?

BIGFOOT'S GOT A LOVER

He was hairy. And tall. A sasquatch down from the mountain. His tangled mass of hair indistinguishable from his beard. Tufts of thick, brown fur sprouted from his back and shoulders and covered his torso and appendages like wall-to-wall carpeting. Sprawled out on the sand, someone might mistake him for a rug and wipe their feet on him. But people kept their distance. He looked harmless enough, sitting next to me in his SpongeBob swim trunks and listening to Barry Manilow on an old boombox, while he slurped on a raspberry popsicle. When he finished it, he rose from his faded paisley beach towel, did a few lunges and burpees, and then bounded into the ocean with loping strides, leaving a trail of footprints for sunbathers to photograph and submit to National Geographic.

Everybody knows Bumbles bounce, but do Bigfoots float? We all paused what we were doing and squinted out into the sparkling waves, secretly rooting for him to make it or conflictedly hoping he would drown. After a nail-biting minute in which his brown coat bobbed and ducked indeterminately in the waves, one shaggy arm shot into the air, followed by the other, and with perfect backstrokes they hauled him down the shoreline, impervious to the waves.

Next to me, Barry finished singing "Mandy" and started in on "Copacabana." A greatest hits cassette. Some people look down on such compilations, but I appreciated its efficiency. It made me want to get up and dance. And sing. But my skin hadn't seen the sun in six months so my cellulite lacked the disguise of a good tan, and I wasn't as free as the hirsute hominid who now hauled himself through the water in the opposite direction with a flawless breaststroke. I wondered how he'd gotten that way. So free. If it was something he'd had to work at or something forced on him by his ... *condition*. Maybe it had come to him in a flash. Maybe one day he'd been in a coffee shop politely sipping an iced chai latte, hoping his boat shoes and gelled hair and Tommy Hilfiger polo would be enough to fit in with everybody else when management came and asked him once again to please leave the premises, and Bigfoot decided once and for all he'd had enough.

The song was half over. The sasquatch came back onshore and shook the water from his fur. Mothers pulled their children from half-finished sandcastles. Fathers reeled in their fishing lines. People hid the phones that had been mounted on the ends of their arms, but Bigfoot stayed at the shoreline and commenced a series of graceful Tai Chi moves. The phones came back out. *Dong Hai Chuan Serves the Tea*. I knew this one. I did it myself but in my bedroom with the door closed.

Everybody knows humans worry about what other humans think of them, but do Bigfoots care? Surely, we were all pondering that question as we squinted at his matted fur glistening in the sun, some of us hoping against hope he wasn't just an elaborate prank staged by an aspiring YouTuber, others of us bristling with indignation that a member of any sentient species would engage in such outrageous conduct on a public beach.

Meanwhile, it was thirty years later at the Copa. Poor Lola was still wearing the same damn dress she had on the day that bastard Rico shot Tony, and I was still sitting on my towel, looking wistfully around the beach, hoping someone would get up and start the dancing. Surely everyone *wanted to*. And while we were at it, break out singing that final, impassioned chorus about that fabulous, fated nightclub where the whole nasty business went down. *I* could start it. *I* could stand up and start singing. Reach my hand out to the person next to me. And that person could reach their hand out to the person next to them, and pretty soon the whole entire beach would be singing and dancing, and *I* could be the one to start it.

I looked at Bigfoot, currently engrossed in a fluid and focused *Repulse the Monkey*. I could feel my toes tingling. My body on the verge of standing up. Lola had lost her mind and so had I! I got to my knees. Stood up on my towel. Opened my mouth to start singing the last refrain, when a group of teenage boys came running up behind Bigfoot, giant slushies in hand. A collective gasp went through the crowd. I started to say something but hesitated, and then it was too late because the slushies flew, and syrup ran thick like glue down the back of the furry sasquatch, and we all could see as plain as day just who got who.

"Get a wax!" one of the boys hollered, and then they all ran off laughing. Next to me, Barry was warning us not to fall in love, but there were more immediate dangers in life like setting yourself up for humiliation. On a public beach. In front of hundreds of people. I sat back down on my towel. Bigfoot stood motionless for a bit, then trudged back into the water to wash off the slushy. When he finished, he came back to his towel, dripping and downcast. He shook his fur, showering me with droplets of saltwater. I tried to think of something nice to say, but everything sounded stupid when I imagined it coming out of my mouth.

"Copacabana" was over. The tape whirred for a few seconds before Barry started in on "It's a Miracle." I knew this one, too. You usually did with a greatest hits tape. That was the point. I glanced sideways at the sasquatch drying off and packing up his stuff. Then I looked around the beach where people were pretending to get back to their own business but were really just watching him surreptitiously through their sunglasses. I could hardly believe it when I heard myself speak.

"Are you any good at *Reeling the Silk*?" I asked.

Bigfoot finished rolling up his bag of cheese puffs and looked at me. "Well," he replied, rather humbly I thought and with a little less bass than expected, "it's foundational to Tai Chi, so ... *yeah*."

"Well," I continued, clearing my throat and glancing around one more time in hopes that at least a few people had gotten bored and gone back to their own business, but everyone still seemed pretty much riveted, "I ask because I have some trouble with it. I've been watching online videos for pointers, but it just never seems to flow."

"Well, I could show you but…" Bigfoot motioned to the crowd, "you might get doused in slushy."

"I don't care," I replied unconvincingly.

"Well … if you want to …" Bigfoot said and then extended his hairy hand to me. I felt my face flush. Could feel everybody's eyes on me. But I reached up and took hold of his hand.

Bigfoot pulled me to my feet, then took me through the move step-by-step. Everyone's phones reappeared, mounted on the ends of their arms. Barry crooned about spectacles and miracles as the teenage boys returned and stood cross-armed off to the side. I could hear their snickers. Feel my face burn anew. Oblivious or ignoring of it all—I still do not know which—Bigfoot continued to advise me with articulate patience about the position of my hips and the stiffness of my arms.

"Bigfoot's got a lover!" one of the boys taunted, but I just kept reeling the silk. Bigfoot wasn't my lover. That was ridiculous. *But*, I thought, as our arms moved in synchronicity before hundreds of mocking, documenting cameras, he was very possibly my savior.

❁

DISCUSSION QUESTIONS

1 Why does the narrator feel wistful as she listens to Copacabana on Bigfoot's cassette? What does the narrator envision happening on the beach as she listens to Copacabana play?

2 Why might the author have chosen an old cassette player for Bigfoot instead of modern technology? Has technology made it easier or harder to be authentic?

3. The narrator imagines that Bigfoot might have had to "work" at being so free. Have you ever tried to care less about others' opinions? What steps did you take, and were they successful?
4. The narrator wonders how Bigfoot had become so free. "If it was something he'd had to work at or something forced on him by his ... condition." What do you think the narrator means by Bigfoot's "condition?"
5. How might Bigfoot serve as a "savior" for the narrator?
6. Do you have someone in your life who reminds you of Bigfoot? How do they make you feel, and what qualities do they possess?
7. What aspects of the story seem liminal to you? (Consider setting, characters, and action.) Is there a liminal guide, and if so, what is the nature of their interaction with other characters?

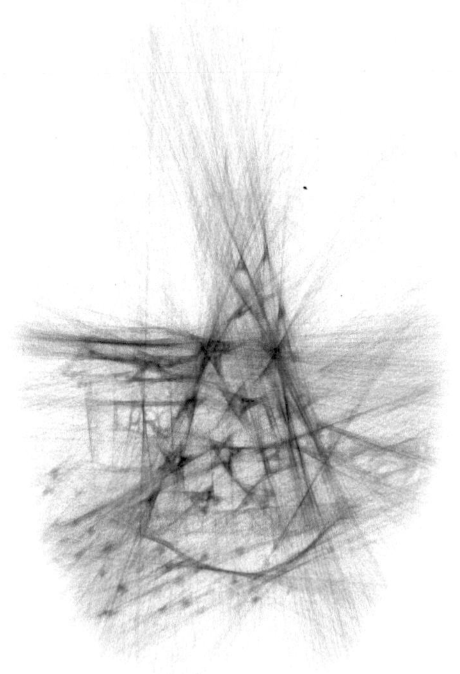

PRE-READING QUESTIONS

- How would you feel if you learned that your birthday was canceled for the rest of your life? Why do you think you would feel this way?
- Would you like it if an entire town celebrated you once in your lifetime?
- Have you ever been in a situation where you pretended to enjoy something for the sake of others? Why did you do this?

THE BIRTHDAY PARTY

It was Archie McGinn's sixtieth birthday, so he slept in. No one expected him to set an alarm. Not on his sixtieth. He could stay in bed as long as he wanted. He didn't even have to show up for work, and everywhere he went people would know it was his birthday. If he had a wife or kids, they might have brought him breakfast in bed, but Archie had neither, so the Sixtieth Birthday Committee sent the neighborhood children over around ten in the morning with a tray of eggs, sausage, hash browns, croissants, and a bowl of what appeared to be his very own blackcaps. They sang him "Happy Birthday" and then ran off hollering, "See you tonight!"

Archie waved after them and hollered back his thanks, then sat down at the kitchen table and popped a few blackcaps into his mouth. He took a big bite of his eggs and chewed while he stared at the cheery, tented place card in front of his orange juice, which read, "Happy Birthday!" Someone had drawn a little flower in the corner. Probably Connie Ellis, who lived just a stone's throw down the street. She never missed a chance to participate in every way possible in a sixtieth birthday. Probably made his breakfast too. Probably picked the blackcaps from the trellis he'd built over the entrance to his front walk. She would most certainly be at his party tonight, making sure she was front and center. It's how it was for the last sixtieth birthday party, and for the one before that, and the one before that.

Archie shoveled a steaming forkful of hash browns into his mouth, and then three more before he thought how he should slow down and savor it. He'd never been very good at that kind of thing though. Always thinking about what was next. It was what he was doing now. Thinking about the stroll he was going to take downtown later and how everyone would come out and wave, and how he'd be invited in for a free shave and haircut at the barber and a piece of pie at the corner restaurant.

Nobody knew for sure who started the sixtieth birthday celebrations. Some said they had begun right there in their own town and spread across the country. But other towns made similar claims. Archie was of the minority opinion that the same idea had probably sprung up at the same time in multiple locations across the country, circumstances being what they were.

When he finished breakfast, Archie took a shower. As he dried himself off, he realized he had intended but failed to savor the hot water running over his skin, the steam opening up his sinuses, and the scent of the bergamot soap diffusing in the damp bathroom air. He considered taking another shower to remedy this inattention, but decided, in the end, that his mind would just run away again on some other track, making it a waste of time.

He intended to enjoy the rest of his day, however. To look at old photos and fix the back porch light. To water the flowers and listen to his favorite songs. But, again, he ended up flitting around the house in a distracted, anxious state, fretting about the trip downtown and his party in the evening, and then, before he knew it, it was four o'clock. He hastily made his bed and tidied the kitchen, then hurried out the front door, which he locked, out of habit, though totally unnecessary on your sixtieth birthday.

Archie paused beneath his trellis to eat a few more blackcaps, then turned and looked back at the little house with the green shutters and the yellow siding, at the purple cone flowers and the little stone gnome. He was proud that he'd kept Sarah Sadler's lilacs alive. He'd considered it his duty to her when he'd first moved in. For forty years, they had been her lilac trees and then for thirty-four they had been his. He hoped that whoever got the house after him would feel a similar sort of loyalty and keep alive not only her lilacs but his blackcaps as well.

The sun was already making its slow descent as Archie hurried downtown. His neighbors had put out their assorted signs, which declared in various cheery colors, "Happy Birthday Archie!" If you didn't look too closely, you couldn't really notice the outlines of other names that had been blotted out and covered with your own. A few neighbors went the extra mile with helium balloons and streamers. One neighbor even got out the Christmas lights and another stuck pink flamingos all over her yard. Some thoughtless brute, new to the neighborhood, stuck a faceless male mannequin with a grass skirt and bedazzled birthday hat in his front yard and called it a day. Across the street, in her yard down on the corner, Connie Ellis was out weeding the flowerbeds with her daughter Savannah, who still lived with her after all these years. Draped from the posts of their white picket fence, a small banner declared, "Happy Birthday Archie!"

"Good evening, Archie!" Connie hollered and waved when she caught sight of him.

"Good evening!" he hollered back. It would be polite to pause and chat for a while, but it agitated him to think how she would behave at his party later that night.

Connie wiped the sweat from her brow, plastered with the damp gray strands of her hair. "You like your breakfast? I picked some of your very own blackcaps for the occasion."

"Yes, thank you!" Archie replied but kept walking, "Good crop of berries this year."

"Must have known it was your sixtieth!" Savannah piped in with a smile.

Archie forced a laugh. It was the kind of thing people liked to say on your sixtieth. He had said such nonsense himself. Archie waved a silent good-bye and quickened his step, but Connie called after him, "I'm making some jam out of 'em, special just for you tonight!"

"Sounds good!" Archie hollered back, "See you then!"

Downtown, things were ramping up. A banner was being strung across the old train bridge over Main Street. "Happy 60th Birthday Archie!" it read and beneath that in smaller letters, "Party Tonight 7–12 at the Old Town Hall. Everyone Welcome!" The town always provided a brand-new banner.

Nothing painted or taped over. He appreciated that, but they also always included the "60th" part. He'd never thought much about it before but seeing it now on his own banner tied his stomach in a knot.

"Archibald McGinn!" Amit Davis called out from behind his barber pole. "It's getting so late, I thought you skipped out on your free shave and haircut!"

"Of course not!" Archie declared, though his enthusiasm for the service had waned.

The barber smiled widely, escorted him to the chair in the front window and put an apron around his neck. There wasn't much to cut as Archie had been in just the week before, but Amit began snipping around anyway at the gray, wispy bits on the top of his head.

Two women stopped outside the window to watch. They smiled and waved to Archie. It made him a little uncomfortable, but he had stopped to watch on other sixtieth birthdays, and there was really nothing you could do about it. Sometimes quite a crowd would assemble, though he hoped it wouldn't be the case today. Archie waved back. With eyes fixed on him and smiles fixed on their faces, the women began talking to each other while pretending they weren't. The front door was propped open, however, and Archie could hear every word they were saying.

"Can you believe how Connie took over the entire event again? It's like we don't even need a Birthday Committee anymore," the woman in the red dress complained.

Archie was gratified to hear he wasn't the only one who felt that way.

The woman in the green hat replied, "Well, if the committee gives that poor spinster daughter of hers the house, you won't have to deal with Connie anymore."

"True, true, but, you know, she deals with that other unpleasant business too, so the committee has been reluctant to let go of her ... *involvement.*"

"Oh ... yes. A bit of a pickle, eh?"

The women waved enthusiastically to Archie and then took off down the street. Amit began trimming around his left ear. Archie hoped he'd be done before anyone else showed up, but three boys pulled up on their bikes.

"Is that *him*?" the littlest boy asked.

"Yeah," replied one of the older boys, the stick of a blow pop hanging out the side of his mouth. "Just think ..." he mused, "someday ... it's gonna be one of us."

The other boy, older too, with long, bleached bangs scoffed, "Never gonna be me—I got somewhere I'm gonna go."

The small boy scrunched up his freckled nose. "You can do that?"

"Hell yeah," he replied, then spat on the ground and tossed back his bangs.

"There isn't anywhere you can go ..." the boy with the blow pop retorted, "it's the same everywhere."

"Your brother doesn't know crap," the boy with the bangs said to the little one. "I saw a movie about a guy who built his own cabin out in the wilderness and lived there until he was 82!"

"That was centuries ago, idiot," the other boy scoffed. "There aren't any places like that left. Don't you pay attention in school?"

The smaller boy frowned at the boy with the bangs, "But you'd miss your party."

"I don't want a stupid party," he sneered.

"There isn't anywhere you can go ..." the older brother repeated.

His friend laughed and took off on his bike. Archie could hear him yell as he rode away down Main Street, "Well, I already got a place, so who's the idiot, now?"

The little brother studied Archie for a bit, then looked up at his brother, confused, "You want a party, right, Jack?"

"Sure," his brother said, tousling the little boy's hair.

"And a shave and a haircut ... and free pie?"

Archie leaned forward, waiting for the older brother's reply. Amit snipped needlessly at the hair around his right ear, as a struggle worked itself out on the boy's face. At last, he replied with a half-hearted smile, "Sure, buddy ... I'll take it all."

Archie leaned back, and the brothers took off on their bikes. He could see a large crowd crossing the street to come and watch, and, all of a sudden, the ties of the apron felt like a noose around his neck. Archie shot up out of the chair and ripped off the apron.

"Thank you, Amit!" he said, forcing another smile.

"But," the barber protested, "the town paid for a haircut *and* a shave."

Archie paused. He had never known that the town paid for the service. He wasn't sure why it mattered, but it made him want to leave all the more.

"Is it customary to tip on ... such a day?" he asked, but seeing the fluster on Amit's face, Archie instantly regretted the question and fumbled around in his pocket for his wallet. He extracted the lone twenty-dollar bill and shoved it into the barber's hand.

"Thank you!" Amit hollered down the street as Archie fled the shop. "I'll make sure everybody knows what a good sport you were on your sixtieth!"

Archie hurried down the block, trying to catch a glimpse of the bang-flipping boy but also being careful to nod and smile at all the well-wishers he passed along the way. At last, when he was almost to the end of Main Street, Archie caught sight of him riding his bike up the West Hill. He hurried after him, but someone grabbed hold of his arm. Archie wheeled around, alarmed, his face just inches from the fat, grinning face of Tobias Dodd, the perpetually sweaty sole proprietor of the corner restaurant.

"You weren't gonna skip out on your pie, today, were ya?" he asked.

Archie squinted up the hill, the boy now just a speck in the distance, then looked around at the expectant, smiling crowd he had tried to dodge at the barber.

"You gotta eat your pie!" someone shouted. There was a

grinning murmur of assent and then the movement of the crowd toward him, until he was ushered inside to the table at the front window. As many as could crowded around, while those who couldn't get close enough assembled outside the window, smiling and waving at him and whispering to one another.

"Coconut cream made fresh this morning!" Tobias announced. He slid a plate with an enormous piece of the pie in front of him. Archie looked down at it, a wide smile plastered on his face. He didn't really like coconut cream pie. In fact, he didn't really like pie at all.

"Thank you," Archie said through his stretched grin, "but I was thinking I might have a cheeseburger instead."

The grinning jack-o'-lantern of Tobias's face dissolved into a squashed pumpkin. A hush fell on the crowd, and the smiles flitted from their faces.

"Well, you see ..." the sole proprietor in him explained while dabbing his perspiring forehead with a handkerchief, "the cheeseburger's three dollars more ... and the town has only paid for the pie ..."

Since Archie had given his twenty to Amit, he didn't have three dollars more, so he forced his smile even wider. "Gotchya there, didn't I?" He winked and took a big bite of the pie. Relief washed over the crowd, and everyone laughed. The baker let out a loud guffaw.

"You almost had me!" Tobias cried, then slapped Archie hard on the back.

"That's a good sport, Archie!" various townspeople said and patted him on the shoulder as he choked down the pie. He was about to force down another bite when he had an idea.

"Bring out some more forks!" Archie yelled, "I'm sharing today!"

This sent a ripple of appreciative, approving murmurs throughout the crowd. Amit sent his daughter Tabitha—the prettiest young woman in town rumored to be pregnant with the child of the very married Housing Committee chair—to get some forks. After a brief commotion, the rest of his pie was distributed, and Archie was no longer obliged to stay. He got up to leave but when he saw Tobias standing by expectantly, he panicked because he had no cash left for a tip. He thought for a few, frazzled seconds, then took off his watch and held it out with both hands.

"Out of gratitude, I would like to give you something very dear to me. My grandfather's gold watch. It keeps impeccable time still to this day."

Tobias looked unsure. "Gold you say, eh?"

"14 karat."

Tobias thought for a moment more, then grinned, took the watch, and shook Archie's hand. "Thank you—and I'll make sure everybody knows what a good sport you were on your sixtieth!"

Someone asked, "Whatchya gonna do until your party tonight, Archie?"

"Well, I thought I'd go for a little walk, get some time alone. But I'll see you all tonight!" He managed a hearty, dismissive wave, and though everyone seemed a little confused, the crowd parted for him, and he hurried down the rest of Main Street, unhindered, toward the West Hill.

There were fewer birthday messages for him in this other neighborhood, but several residents had still made an effort with signs and balloons. Some thoughtful child had painted a life-size picture of him but hung it from the branch of a tree, where it dangled in the wind. Archie hurried past. He thought he heard voices then, so he glanced behind him. A whole trail of people followed. They waved and smiled, but he pretended not to notice and trudged up the hill with urgent strides. More and more people appeared in their front yards, hollering out to him as he passed, "Happy birthday, Archie!" and "See you soon!"

At last, Archie reached the top of the hill. At the end of a cul-de-sac the mayor's mansion soared and sprawled ten times larger than any other house in town. The boy's bike lay in the front yard. He glanced behind him. The crowd had not yet crested the hill. He hurried up the walk and knocked on the door. The mayor answered.

"Well, hello Mr. McGinn and happy birthday! I was just getting ready for your party." She wore a bright purple dress and large, gold earrings. In his jeans and faded flannel, Archie felt underdressed. "What can I do for you?" she asked. She was young. Somewhere in her thirties. She couldn't possibly understand. He would keep it vague.

"Well, ma'am," he replied, parched and out of breath, I'm looking for the boy who was riding that bike."

"My Charlie? Whatever for?"

"I just want to ask him something. It'll only take a minute." The crowd had caught up and stood unsure now in the middle of the cul-de-sac. The mayor looked at them over Archie's shoulder. A troubled look passed across her face but then mutated into a bright smile.

"But of course. It is your *sixtieth* after all. He's in the gazebo out back," she said, pointing toward the side of the house.

"Thank you, ma'am," Archie said, then hurried around back. When he got there, however, he stopped dead in his tracks, mesmerized by what he saw—a yard ten times the size of any in town and filled with mighty old oaks and towering pines. There were no such trees in the rest of the town. Only manageable ones that wouldn't heave up the sidewalk or fall on your neighbor's house. Ones that could fit in your postage stamp-size lawn. But he wouldn't complain. Not now. They had it good in their little town. Some faraway countries with archaic laws didn't even have houses anymore. Or lawns. Just highrise after highrise filled with coffin-sized bunks. Even so, he *must* talk to Charlie. Archie hurried toward the gazebo.

"Who's there?" the boy called, then poked his head out to see. "Oh ... you," he said, then added unconvincingly, "Happy birthday."

"Thank you," Archie replied, glancing behind him. The mayor was making her way toward them with something to drink. He didn't have much time. "Say," he whispered, "the place you were telling the boys about ... the place you're going to go? Where is it?"

The boy's eyes narrowed, then widened. "Oh..." he stammered, as his face reddened, "Well, it's ... *here.*"

"What?" Archie asked, uncomprehending.

The boy glanced over Archie's shoulder at his mother, who was almost upon them. He leaned forward and whispered. "I'm gonna be mayor someday and, once I'm here, I'm *never* gonna leave."

Archie stared, still uncomprehending, but then the mayor was next to him with her smile and iced tea, and Archie began to laugh. He laughed and laughed, and he couldn't stop. A nervous titter escaped the mayor's lips, and she called for her husband in a strained tone.

"No need, Madam Mayor," Archie said, stumbling backwards. "I've inconvenienced you all long enough!" He turned and fled the scent of the pines and the shade of the oaks and the Grecian gazebo and the mayor's foolish, foolish boy. Back out front, the crowd had tripled in size.

"There's the man of the day!" someone yelled, and they all rushed at him. He was lifted and carried above their heads all the way back down the hill as they sang at the top of their lungs, "For he's a jolly good fellow, for he's a jolly good fellow, for he's a jolly good fellow, which nobody can deny!"

They brought him right through the front doors of the Old Town Hall, where Connie Ellis was fussing over the buffet table. A band struck up a polka tune, and little children dressed in their very best blew into their noisemakers as hard as they could. The crowd deposited Archie on the birthday throne, strapped a birthday hat to his head, and handed him a birthday mug full of beer.

Archie preferred whiskey, but he knew beer was more affordable for the town. He wouldn't ask. He drank the first one down because it was his party, and when he was handed another, he drank that one down too, because there wasn't anywhere else to go. Someone brought him a third beer then, and he drank until he was in a stupor because he didn't know what else to do.

Connie brought him over a plate of food. "Now you enjoy

that, Archie," she said, "but save a little room for some jam later. I made it special just for *you* tonight." She smiled and went back to the buffet where she oversaw the refilling of platters and the administering of the keg. Archie gobbled down his food and then got it in his head to get up and dance. It was, as he had already reminded himself, his party, and there wasn't anywhere else to go, and he didn't know what else to do. The townspeople pushed him into the middle of the crowd, and he started doing a jig. They made a circle around him and clapped and hooted, and then, when another tune started up, the lovely Tabitha Dodd danced a polka around the room with him.

When the dance was over, the room was spinning. He almost fell over, but the crowd swooped in and lifted him once again above their heads, chanting "Archie! Archie!" and deposited him back on the throne, where Connie waited for him with a jam-filled croissant. Another polka tune started up, and the crowd went back to dancing.

"Here you go, Archie," Connie said, holding the croissant out to him. He opened his mouth to take a big bite, but she smiled kindly at him and it made him pause—for the night was still young and there were more jigs to dance and beers to drink and beautiful women to whisk around the hall. Seeing his hesitation, she added, "Just a little something to get you through."

Archie *was* hungry. A good jig worked up an appetite. He bit half of it off and chewed with vigor.

"That's right," Connie said with tender eyes. "Jam made with berries you cultivated all these years with so much care. I tried to make it special for you, Archie. I always try to make it special."

Archie nodded appreciatively and took the croissant, so buttery and sweet with the jam, and shoved the rest of it into his mouth. As he swallowed the last bite, he began to feel sleepy.

"That's right," Connie said again, taking his hand as his head plunked against the back of the birthday throne. Her eyes grew moist and her lips quivered. At first Archie didn't understand what was happening but then he did, and his eyes went wide in terror.

She squeezed his hand. "It's all right, Archie. I fixed things so you can just go to sleep. I've got everything in hand. You just go to sleep now, okay?"

Archie wanted to go to sleep and yet he didn't. He shouldn't! But her lips trembled, and the moistness of her eyes brimmed on her lashes, and somehow it made it all right. His terror gave way. Archie closed his eyes and let the tiredness wash over him. As he drifted off, he thought of the begonias he hadn't watered and the porch light he hadn't fixed and how glad he was that a person like Connie Ellis had everything in hand.

Connie stood beside Archie for the remaining half-hour of the party, holding his hand. People began to leave once they saw her standing there. They smiled and waved and called "Goodbye!" to Archie from a distance, pretending he wasn't already a corpse.

The Housing Committee decided that Archie's house should go to Tabitha Dodd, who moved in the nexut morning. Connie watched from her yard as Tabitha passed under the trellis and hummed her way to the front door. She didn't mind at all that the house had gone to Tabitha. uConnie liked having her daughter at home, and she only had four years left with her.

❁

DISCUSSION QUESTIONS

1 Three boys on bikes talk about the birthday celebration—the boy with the bleached bangs mentions that he plans to skip his birthday celebration and go somewhere else. How does the boy with the blow pop react?

2 What question does the little boy ask his older brother after the boy with the bleached bangs leaves? How does the older brother respond?

3 How does Archie's request for a cheeseburger instead of pie affect the townspeople? Why do you think they react this way? Why do you think he ends up eating the pie instead of the cheeseburger?

4 How does the mayor's yard differ from those of the other citizens? How does Archie imagine his town compares to other towns?

5 Did you start feeling something bad was going to happen at the birthday party? When? Why?

6 How does Archie feel about his neighbor Connie at the beginning of the story? How does he feel about her at the end? How did your feelings change about her over the course of the story?

7 What do you think of the town's housing/population arrangement? Would you want to live in such a community, or would you try to find somewhere else to go?

8 What do you think of Connie's involvement in the party? What do you think of the townspeople's involvement?

9 If you lived there, would you participate in the 60th birthday parties? If so, why? How?

10 What aspects of the story seem liminal to you? (Consider setting, characters, and action.) Is there a liminal guide, and if so, what is the nature of their interaction with other characters?

PRE-READING QUESTIONS

- Do you often remind yourself that you're going to die one day? Do you think that's a helpful or harmful habit? How might this reminder change your attitude toward your day?

THE STRETCH MOTEL

A WAD OF CHEWING TOBACCO BULGES BEHIND FRANCINE'S bottom lip as she presses a Gideon into my palm and says, "You know, Jimmy, you're gonna die someday."

I look down at the little green book, vinyl-bound with fake gold letters. We put 'em in every nightstand, along with a dog-eared coupon for Angelino's Pizza and a color postcard for the Klassy Gents Klub. The Stretch Motel is all about options.

"And that someday might be soon," she adds, spitting into the dandelions that sprawl out of the cracks in the curb.

"Francine," I reply with a raised eyebrow, "you're not thinking of having a hand in that, are ya?"

She grins, flecks of tobacco clinging to her yellow teeth. Brown juice oozes up to the top of her bottom lip, and I wonder why she's bringing up death so goddam early in the morning. She unlocks the next room.

Cleaning motel rooms isn't hard, per se. You rip off the sheets and put on a new set. Swipe down the toilet and the sink—no need to bleach anything, just make it look good. Stash the bathroom with clean towels, fresh soap, and those little shampoo and conditioner bottles everybody takes home and leaves in their medicine cabinet for the next six years 'til they finally throw 'em out, unused. Dust the furniture with a generic orange-scented wax product. Wipe the windows with a generic lemon-scented glass cleaner. Vacuum if necessary. Make sure the coupon, the card, and the Gideon are neatly arranged in the drawer, bottoms together, tops fanned out. Rotate the one that's on top if you're unsure, like me, which option you prefer.

We're just about to step into Room 176, when we hear tires squeal into the parking lot. We hurry down to the end of the 170s and lean out around the corner, bracing ourselves against the wind gusting off the semis that whiz down the interstate. It's so damn bright we can't make out the vehicle, so we shield our eyes in synchronicity, like recruits saluting the flag. A boxy, brown Buick LeSabre with out-of-state plates pulls up to one of the cheapest rooms nearest the highway. A room so damn loud you can't help but picture poor insomniac bastards flipping through the channels late at night, the fake pine paneling closing in around 'em, as they reach for the nightstand drawer.

Order pizza.

Call a girl.

Get saved.

No one's really sure which way to go, so you try a little of each, and then, as Francine has reminded me for some goddam reason today, you die.

So, there we are, leaning out past the 170s, looking like we're saluting the vehicles barreling down the interstate transporting products to people who don't need 'em and people to vacations that won't make 'em happy. My faded but favorite Metallica shirt plasters against my scrawny torso, and my hair whips against my face. The door of the LeSabre opens. A lumpy, middle-aged woman in stage makeup and a red sequin dress gets out. She tries to hold her bleached updo in place, but her Aqua Net Extra Super Hold is no match for the barrage of 18-wheelers. A door opens. Room 184. With a glance at one another, we acknowledge this fact. A fact relevant to no one else, and to us for no other reason than the camaraderie of communal workplace knowledge. We resume our vigil. A gray, lanky man in white gloves and a faded tuxedo drags a guillotine out of the room with one hand and grips his top hat to his head with the other. The woman lets one side of her hair go to help him. They wrestle the contraption into the backseat, the car doors occasionally blowing shut during the ordeal, hitting 'em both in the ass. I don't think to help. I just stand and stare, ruminating on the four of us there, our hands glued to our heads, fortressing ourselves against the forces of nature and technology, contemplating our shared humanity and shit, when Francine snaps me with a spring-breeze scented trash bag, and I follow her back to 176. I grab clean, folded sheets from the cart.

"Your turn to do the bathroom," she reminds me.

"Oh yeah," I mumble, then shove the sheets back onto the cart. Francine thrusts the bathroom bucket into my hands.

"Can we take a cigarette break after this one?" I ask because she's in charge and, even though we had a cigarette break just two rooms ago, I can usually get her to cave if I offer her one of my Newports.

She turns toward me with a look of exasperation. "You wanna die, Jimmy?"

"What's all this talk about death all the goddam sudden?"

She puts her hand on her bulbous hip, pulling her faded blue smock tight across her equally bulbous stomach. "I just think you need to make some changes. Quit smokin' for starters."

"You smoke!"

"I know. But that doesn't mean you should. I'm old and all I've got is my shows, my Little Caesars, and my tobacco."

I'm silent because I feel bad that she can't afford the swankier pie from Angelino's, even with the goddam coupon. I feel bad about her whole life presented as such.

"Hey," I say, remembering a pertinent fact, "you gotchyer cat, right?"

"I suppose..." Francine says and sprays the white rag with the orange-scented polish. She begins wiping down the Formica dresser. "But anybody can put food in a bowl twice a day and empty a litter box."

"And you got your job here. You manage housekeeping for this whole damn place. It would be a nasty fuckin' dump if I was in charge."

"Well, if *you* were in charge, sure," she says, all matter-of-fact, not even aware she's being offensive, when I was being all nice and shit, "but there's a lot of people out there who can make sure seventy rooms get cleaned by 6:00 p.m. every night."

She has a point. One which nags me pretty regular. Especially when I'm hauling my ass out of bed at six in the morning to walk 1.2 miles to the sprawling decline of the Stretch Motel, so my stepdad doesn't kick my graduated ass out to the curb.

Francine starts stripping the beds. Double queens. I go into the bathroom and survey the grossness. I give it a 3 out of 10, with 10 being vomit on the floor or shit on the wall, which I get more regular than you'd think. I never got a dead body though. That would be at least a 25.

"I watched your cat once, remember?" I call out suddenly from the bathroom, where I'm leaned over, swishing the brush half-heartedly in the toilet. "When you were in the hospital for that heart thing."

"Yeah?" she says, huffing as she snaps a clean sheet out over one of the beds.

"Well," I holler over the flushing of the toilet, "He wouldn't eat any of his food while you were gone. He just meowed the whole goddam time and sat by the door."

Francine doesn't say anything. I lean out of the bathroom, the toilet brush dripping into the carpeting.

"He would forget me eventually," she says, fluffing a pillow. She waddles over to the other side of the bed. She needs both knees replaced but can't afford to take off work. Or the three thousand dollar co-pay. She needs to lose eighty pounds but can't give up Little Caesars. Or Dairy Queen. A double-bind common in these parts. "Besides," she adds, "he might be better off with someone else, anyway."

"I can't even believe you just said that. Pets die all the fuckin' time out of loneliness for their human companions."

Francine looks uncertain as she creases the bedspread beneath the pillows. I, myself, am not sure if this is true. Don't people go on, all the time? After their cats die? Their dogs die? Mr. Vogel kept showing up to school every day to teach chemistry after his six-year-old son died of goddam leukemia, teaching shitheads sleeping in the back of class, attending pep rallies and discussing B minuses at teacher conferences like any of it mattered anymore. But isn't that life? Going the fuck on?

I touch up the mirror while Francine runs the vacuum behind me. I look at her reflection, her sweat beading on a moustache more conspicuous than anything I've yet to produce, and wonder if I, too, will be traipsing to the faded rooms of the Stretch Motel until I need both knees replaced, my decades on earth marked by the toilets I've scrubbed and the queen beds I've made. She unplugs the vacuum, and I shut off the air conditioning. We step outside, and I pass her a Newport. We huddle in the doorway and light our smokes.

"*Three* rooms before the next one," Francine says, then inhales long and hard.

I nod, but I know she'll cave. Francine squints across the parking lot like she's studying some molecule of air. Most days on our smoke breaks, she updates me on the love quadrangles and betrayals and impassioned reunions in the shows she records every day and watches every night, but, today, we stand there in silence, breathing in the exhaust from the highway and the stench from the sewage plant, savoring every draw on our cancer sticks. We hear tires squeal again in the side parking lot and look at each other. I grin and bolt to see what's what.

"Checkout 184!" I announce as the LeSabre peels out. I tap my cigarette butt with the worn toe of last year's gym shoe because Francine will worry if I don't, even though they paved paradise for a goddam mile in any direction you look, and I don't think it would be any great tragedy if the Stretch Motel, hobbling for decades toward its final expiration date, were to suddenly make its exit in a defiant blaze of glory.

Francine looks at her watch and says, "I told you they'd be late."

"You did," I say. "Ya call it every time. They're just lucky we didn't pound on their door half-an-hour ago, shoutin' '*Housekeeping, motherfuckers!*' "

This gets a small smile out of Francine, who tosses her cigarette on the sidewalk and stomps its microscopic embers out with the thick sole of her black shoe.

"You think they left a tip?" she asks.

"Nope."

"You always say that."

"Yep. And I always believe it with all my heart. That way, I won't be disappointed. But, if there *is* one, I'll be surprised. And happy. And I'll do your favorite dance." I start headbanging there on the sidewalk, my stringy brown hair flying up and down like the brushes of a car wash gone mad.

"*A dance?*" she says, hand on her hip and eyebrow raised. A little sass coming back into the old girl.

"Times change," I say, swinging the cart around the corner and rapping, just to be sure, on the door of Room 184. "Ya didn't think the Mashed Potato would be a thing forever, did ya?"

I glance at her, grinning, sure I'd brought her around, but there are tears in the corners of her eyes as she organizes the paper-wrapped soaps in their box. *Shit.* I can see how that maybe wasn't the thing to say. I unlock the door and glance at her again. I'm reaching for the sheets because it's my turn, but then notice something huddling behind the weed-filled flowerpot beneath the window. I crouch down.

"Look," I whisper to Francine. I feel her take a step closer and hover above me.

Francine gasps, "Their magic rabbit!"

"Must have gotten left behind," I say.

"Or escaped!" she whispers. I can feel her excitement. Feel her lean in closer.

"Betchya that rabbit's never spent a day outside," I say, "Betchya he won't last the night. Betchya he'll run up on the interstate and get squashed by a truck."

"We can't leave him here!" Francine declares. "You think you can get him?"

"Maybe," I say, "hand me a sheet."

She passes one to me. I unfold it to quarter size, then pounce on the rabbit.

"Don't hurt it!"

I move fast, secure the sheet around the rabbit, feel it squirm in my hands.

"I've got him!"

Francine presses her hands together and bites her lip, then ushers me into the room. She shuts the door and waddles over to me, eyes wide and panting. I tell her to sit on the bed, and I put the squirming bundle in her arms. She unwraps the sheet carefully and gets hold of its soft white body. Presses it to her sweaty, ample bosom and runs her hand down its back, speaking softly to it. Its red eye stares out, wide and terrified, in my direction. Unsettled by its piercing, one-eyed gaze, I turn away to survey the room damage. Cigarettes overflow in the ashtray. Every goddam light on. No blood or semen in the bed. A discarded but unused condom in the trash. The toilet paper, tissue, lotion, shampoo, and conditioner—*taken*. Bright red lipstick on not one but *two* washcloths. No stolen towels, but the bathroom reeks of hairspray and a fresh dump. At least they flushed. I come back out and check the table and counters.

"No tip," I complain.

"I thought you weren't expectin' one."

"Yeah, but I just don't understand why people don't leave a goddam tip! Would it kill 'em to leave a few bucks? Don't they know people gotta smoke?"

"You should quit anyway," Francine says without looking away from the rabbit, which she has now lifted to her face.

"Well, I will if you will," I say, opening and slamming the dresser drawers shut, hoping that, in lieu of a tip, they might have forgotten something I could sell for a couple of bucks.

"Hey ..." I say to Francine, "how 'bout we make a trip down to the pet store on our lunch break?"

I'm thinking maybe we get ten bucks for the albino, but Francine says, "That's a great idea! I've got a large crate I could turn into a real cozy hutch, but, if this little guy's gonna make it, I've gotta get him some of that Timothy hay."

I look over at Francine, nuzzling the rabbit against her cheek, then open the nightstand drawer in a last hope of finding something I can sell. But there's only the usual array. On the top, the shiny postcard for the Klassy Gents Klub. In the middle, the small green wedge of the Gideon. And, on the bottom, the dog-eared corner of Angelino's goddam useless motherfucking coupon. I sigh quietly and shove the drawer shut with my knee.

"Yeah ..." I say, throwing the frayed bedspread on the floor and springing loose the graying fitted sheet, "if the little guy's gonna make it, you gotta give him what he needs."

❁

DISCUSSION QUESTIONS

1 Jimmy thinks about the options sleepless motel guests face when they turn to their nightstands: What is his attitude toward these different options? What does Jimmy's view of these choices suggest to you about his view of life?

2 What is Jimmy's view of how motel guests use the toiletry products? What does he think about the vacations people take at motels like his?

3 What is the woman wearing when she gets out of the LeSabre? What happens to her hair? Why do you think the author chose to have the woman and a man in a tuxedo put a stage guillotine in the back seat of a car? What does Jimmy think about as he watches the couple struggle in the wind?

4 Why does Francine ask Jimmy if he wants to die? Why do you think Francine gives Jimmy advice about smoking when she is a smoker herself?

5 How does Francine respond when Jimmy tells her he needs her help to keep the motel clean? What point from Francine's speech 'nags at' Jimmy? Why do you think it bothers him?

6. What does Jimmy tell Francine about her cat? Why do you think he tells her this?
7. Jimmy says, "Don't people go on, all the time?" What does he mean by this? What example does he give to support this idea?
8. Why does Jimmy start head-banging? What does he see that makes him second-guess his comment about the mashed potato not being around forever?
9. What does Jimmy think about doing with the rabbit left behind by the guests? Why does Francine want to go to the pet store? What does this suggest to you about Francine?
10. Why do you think the story ends with Jimmy's words: "If the little guy's gonna make it, you gotta give him what he needs?" What do the characters turn out to need in this story? Do you think they get it?
11. What aspects of the story seem liminal to you? (Consider setting, characters, and action.) Is there a liminal guide, and if so, what is the nature of their interaction with other characters?

PRE-READING QUESTIONS

- What would you say is the most dangerous trait a leader can possess? Can you think of any present or historical leaders who exemplify this trait?
- Do you believe modern democracies are functioning effectively? Any specific issues that worry you?

MISTAKES MAY HAVE BEEN MADE

"IT IS A GREAT HONOR IN THIS EXTRAORDINARY HOUR TO address the noble porcine, bovine, hircine, and equine delegations among us. Let the record note the sheer number of representatives from the murine and leporine delegations—the ubiquity of our rat and rabbit friends never ceases to astonish. Let the record also note," Horace added, pausing to assume a grave countenance, "that this honorable assembly is grieved—sorely grieved—at the departure of the canine from our coalition. It was, perhaps, always known deep down in our hearts that their true loyalty lay with the human devils. Nevertheless, it was a loss hard taken. There has since been the bandying about of blame and the sickness of second-guessing spreading like a cancer amongst certain factions of our cause. But let us acknowledge that intentions were good even though mistakes may have been made."

Horace cleared his throat and pushed up his glasses. The delegates looked at him expectantly. Recent events had compelled him, however, to rely more than usual upon that liquid form of courage so dear to the human devils, so he took a moment to stick his snout into his bowl of beer to lap up some of the frothy malt, then snuck another look at the crowd. *Good.* His fellow pigs slurped up their beer as well, taking their cues from him. The horses, of course, stood still and silent behind them, tails twitching meditatively—the *esteemed equine* never imbibed. Or argued. Or cheered. As pacifists, they never did much of anything besides show up out of "solidarity," a useless gesture as far as Horace was concerned. Frankly, they would've served him better, during recent trying events, as dog meat.

"But I dare say," Horace continued with a point he knew to be popular with the masses, "that not a single member of this honorable assembly is distressed at the absence of the feline contingency. No, they were never part of this, by their own desire, it should be remembered. Too good for the rest of us. Too disinterested in the affairs of mortals. No. The felines were never part of this, but they could have been. They could have been part of this critical moment in history when *Animalia omnia* begin, at last, to take their rightful place alongside *Homo sapiens sapiens.*"

Heads nodded all around, and the pleasing murmur of consternated agreement filled the room. One of the bovines mooed, and Horace had to stifle a shudder. They always took the big table in front, blocking the view, masticating right there in front of everybody, mooing when they got too excited about things, forgetting to use their words. And the flatulence. It would linger within the dark, paneled walls of the tavern, infusing the fusty dankness with its fetor. Horace sighed interiorly. No, the bovines had not even been wanted in this coalition—their shared, historical industrial-farming trauma notwithstanding—but they'd been invited, nonetheless, by the asinine delegation, who, in yet another act of contumacious contrariness, had absented themselves from the Weekly Meeting for the drunken, braying funeral bash for Old Mad Jack.

Horace went on. "But this recent setback—the treachery of the tail-wagging traitors—shall not be counted as a loss, my friends. No, it shall be but vital documentation of a living struggle that will endure until its triumph at the designated time—"

The goats broke out in simultaneous bleats of protest, so Horace hastened to add, "of our own choosing!" He smiled emphatically, hoping it had worked. The hircines always took umbrage at any vocabulary that implied order or higher consciousness in the universe. It was a long story but, around the time the horses had gone metaphysical, the goats had gone material. It was the only way, they said, they could make sense of such a brutal world. This was all well and good, to each his own, et cetera, et cetera, but they had the irritating habit of calling Horace out whenever he waxed platonic or veered predestinarian. And to compound vexation with aggravation, they felt the incessant need to clarify to everyone around them that it was the natural sort of materialism to which they adhered, rather than the historical or dialectical. As far as Horace was concerned, however, it was all wasted smelly goat breath, for only horses and pigs could follow such arguments, and the horses had given up philosophical debate and the pigs didn't care about philosophy at all.

But he needn't have worried about a hircine haranguing because the avian delegation arrived just then and swept through the tavern, creating a colossal kerfuffle. Eventually, the sparrows lighted on the windowsill and the starlings settled on the rafters, prompting the pigs to pull their beers in closer. Horace grimaced. He absolutely needed the avians, but that didn't mean he had to like them. Or trust them. With those wings of theirs, they were just too *free*. Who knew where they went when they left the Weekly Meeting? No one could follow them. And they were so condescending, always claiming superior knowledge with their "bird's eye view" of things. Know-it-alls of the absolute worst order and, yet, jealous of his education. Some species just couldn't stand a lettered pig. And the starling faction. *Criminals*. Every last one of them. When Horace first started his university, they'd flown overhead, doing their choreographed stunts and unleashing a blitzkrieg of their bowels upon his students, bullying him into a protection racket in which he'd been trapped ever since. He was so naïve back then, it was entirely possible—though absolutely unprovable since no paper trail existed—that mistakes may have been made.

Horace continued. "Be not overly discouraged by the incident at the mine, my friends. The rumblings of the Reckoning are being heard 'round the world. Fifteen seats have been won on town councils, eight on county boards, and the very first in our own state's assembly!"

The pigs pounded their bowls on the table, sloshing their beer on the floor and their laps. "Hear, hear!" they cried. The starling faction did a fancy swoop through the rafters, both to show off and to make sure they'd been seen by Horace, who still owed them a month's worth of grain. The bovines mooed. The goats, always eager for a chant, shouted, "Doc Bison! Doc Bison!"

Horace forced a smile. It was supposed to have been *him* in the state assembly—Professor Horace Yorkshire, the pig who'd started it all—and, yet, it was Doc Bison's star that had somehow ascended. Sure, there were certain electability issues with Horace. His unfortunate, adolescent endorsement of the Porcines Are People Too campaign. His former affiliation with the now known predator, Wild Boar Bill. His controversial periplaneta agenda. If only the other delegates had been able to see the value of the cockroach constituency, for, outside his students, they had always been his biggest supporters.

"Today the state capitol, tomorrow the presidential palace!" Horace shouted over the din, inciting the crowd to louder, more vigorous cheers.

If only, Horace thought as he plastered a wide smile on his snout and lifted his front feet in the expected but ridiculous devilish gesture of victory, the canines hadn't thrown their weight behind Doc Bison—a mere visiting lecturer *from the Midwest.* And then, to add insult to injury, after securing the nomination for that pompous windbag, those brown-nosing backstabbers had gone sniveling back to the devils. Horace *never* should have trusted them. A few impassioned speeches could never overcome the thousands of years of breeding and conditioning that had duped the dogs into that unholy alliance.

But oh, the agony! Of all the species to double-cross him! It had always been a particular source of bitterness to him that, though they were species of equal intelligence and affection, all those thousands of years ago, the dog had been chosen by those human devils for companionship and the pig for *consumption.* The inequity of it still astounded. *Devils be damned!* Perhaps his zeal for the cause had blinded him to the canines' true allegiance, but, in his defense, he'd been distracted by the ill-timed affair of his wife with the handsome, virile boar from the south—*his own graduate student*—and, in such a stupor as he was at the time, mistakes may have been made.

"The fight will never be abandoned," Horace continued, "until every living being on this planet has a voice in how it is run. Suffrage for all!"

The goats took up one of their impassioned but ill-crafted chants, "Speedboat the vote! Speedboat the vote!" An unpleasant bleating erupted from a pubescent billy, but his father headbutted him into silence.

Just then, the face of one of the human devils appeared in the window. Its horrid mouth opened and cried, "Justice for the plant world!"

The sparrows who'd been gossiping on the windowsill panicked and took flight inside the tavern, maneuvering in chaotic dips and reversals, causing mayhem in the crowd. The starlings took the opportunity to defecate in everyone's beer, and a long, loud expulsion of methane erupted from a sheepish looking cow.

"Suffrage for all means suffrage for *all!*" the devil shouted.

Where were the cockroaches when you needed them? Disgusting though they may be, an army of them would come in handy about now. But he hadn't seen their leader, Crich, for days. Not since Horace's "57-Point Plan for the Peaceful Cohabitation of Periplaneta With People" had been leaked. Perhaps Horace should have come down harder in the plan on the use of pesticides and gone easier on the repugnant habits of the roaches. Perhaps, when Crich had confronted him about it, he shouldn't have tried to pass it off as fake news, since everybody knew that tactic only worked on the devils. Horace sighed but consoled himself with the knowledge that at least he was the kind of leader who could admit to himself that—in pursuit of the higher good, which was, truthfully, best secured through the advancement of his own political career—mistakes may have been made.

Meanwhile, the rats had taken advantage of the commotion to sneak off to the kitchen, while the rabbits struggled to keep their children in line. Why they didn't just hire babysitters, Horace would never understand. The sparrows settled on the old piano, and one of the horses opened the door to let the methane out. The starlings sat smugly on a beam above. The devil was gone from the window but had left a potted maple on the sill with a placard that read, "Trees are Life!"

"Someone remove that pot!" Horace ordered, affecting concern for the feelings of the cows who had read the sign and now sunk lower in their seats. Everyone knew the sordid history of the two species—the cows had almost destroyed the earth in the 21st century and the trees had saved it. It didn't matter that it was the devils who had purged the earth of its greatest air purifiers and who had multiplied the number of these misshapen, mooing, methane machines to mythological orders of magnitude—the *cows* felt the shame of it. Worse than any branding the devils had ever done in the flesh of any bovine was the branding of history. It was true that Horace could do more to lift the burden of shame they collectively carried, but it was also true that it provided a certain political advantage to him if they carried it. It kept them eager to please, grateful to be included. In short, it meant votes. And though mistakes may have been made along the way, this was most certainly not one of them.

Horace opened his mouth to continue his speech, but something caught his attention. A shifting of shadows on the side wall. A protracted, whispered rush that made everyone's spine tingle, followed by a silent, hair-raising moment in which Horace recalled an ominous visit he'd received that morning from a delegation of Daddy Longlegs who'd made the long treacherous journey from the nation's capital. He'd forgotten all about it, so many important things he had to do that day—preparations for the Weekly Meeting, an upcoming national election, his regular afternoon tryst with the sassy sow from the sociology department—but now, the single, airy, elongated syllable of which their entire message was comprised came back to him in haunting cadence. "Bombs!" they'd said over and over again, unable to provide any context because they never bothered to master the lingua franca—just *bombs*, delivered as though from the mouths of a Greek chorus. Then they'd departed as silently as they'd come.

Horace wondered if perhaps there was some connection, thought for a moment he should maybe share the information, but he had no corroborating intelligence, couldn't afford any more political fallout, and, in the end, even if he had wanted to, he was unable to because a red speckled hen squawked, "It's the ghost of Old Mad Jack!"

This declaration sent the rest of the chickens running at random angles with no apparent destination, and an unpleasing murmur of consternated agreement filled the room. Horace gritted his teeth. As with the cows, he'd put up with the hens for the sake of their shared subjugation to the horrors of industrial farming, but the ignorance and superstition he'd had to endure! The unrelenting frustration as their pebble-sized brains habitually failed to grasp the larger picture. Case in point: If Old Mad Jack died in service of the cause he believed in—if the old ass fell headfirst into a shaft of the mine he may have been asked to blow up and broke all four legs and his neck in the process—Old Mad Jack would understand, postmortem—no matter what hircine philosophy had to say about the matter—that it was all for the good of the cause. And any creature who had a brain larger than a pea would know that under such circumstances of mutual understanding and camaraderie the old donkey would most certainly not come back to haunt them!

At least his fellow pigs understood. They knew what was at stake. What had to be done. Horace looked at them now, his faithful students leaning over their bowls of beer at their table in the back. Their subtle nods and wide-eyed admiration always gave him courage, but looking at them now, Horace faltered and felt the warm flush of shame as it occurred to him they might be privy to his wife's indiscretions with the famed, former boar stud who now taught them "The Principles of Marketing." That their wide eyes were not an indication of their admiration at all, but a fixed sort of glaze meant to obscure their new, true feelings.

Horace began to tremble. He leaned over his bowl to lap up the rest of his beer, but a large white lump of excrement floated in it. Perhaps, his students knew that it had been he, in a crazed fit of rage and indignation, who had pseudonymously penned the articles in the *Gazette*, questioning Doctor Bison's credentials and undermining the credibility of the election. Mistakes such as these may have been made but—*the ghost of Old Mad Jack be damned*—Horace was certainly not responsible for any of them. He was victim to forces beyond his control—the changing winds of politics, the unthinking mental migrations of the herd, accidents and infidelities, the black swans of life that could make or break a movement or a leader—and he didn't care about that seat in the lowly state assembly anyway. He would run for President—*the Professor of the Plains, his whore of a wife, his ingrate of a graduate student, the canines and the felines and the bovines and the hircines and the whole damned lot of them be damned!*

Meanwhile, the cockroach delegation scurried away from the tavern where they'd been listening from the crevices of the paneling. It hadn't been the ghost of Old Mad Jack at all that had sent shivers down the spines of the others, but the horde, exiting en masse when Crich gave the signal. They always did exactly what Crich told them. They believed in him, and that was all that was needed to get them through the events that were about to unfold. He would explain things to them tomorrow. After it happened. But should he forewarn the termites? Should he share with them the message passed along to him from his 18th cousin twice removed, living in the warm walls of the Presidential Palace? Crich pondered it all as the horde scuttled after him across the ditch and through the moldering leaves. He certainly wasn't going to tell Horace and the others now. It was bad enough they hadn't cancelled the Weekly Meeting to attend the old donkey's funeral, but not a single word of respect? No moment of silence? Sure, Old Mad Jack was an ass, but he was a *good* ass. He, alone, had the common decency to share Horace's degrading "57-Point Plan" with him.

As far as Crich was now concerned they were *all* devils and, *all the devils be damned*, he and his kind would survive. They'd already survived 320 million years and they'd survive 320 million more, *nuclear winter be damned*. The roaches would inherit the earth! Though, apparently, the latest research indicated they'd have to share it with the flour beetles, and everybody knew how annoying *they* were. As the horde crawled up under the siding of their two-story and Crich nestled into the best spot in the wall behind the stove, he thought about the message his cousin had sent. The devils were doing it *today*. If there was some way to warn the old devil on the other side of the drywall he might, but any previous overtures of friendship had been greeted with a spray can and a broom. No, Crich would just sleep now and rise to a new world order tomorrow. He would have to give a speech, of course. Perhaps in the basement of the old schoolhouse where thousands of the horde would already be congregated. He would lay out a six-point plan—six points because he liked the number six, because cockroaches had six legs—a six-point plan that would outline the future of their world. He felt excited just thinking about it. And a little guilty too, especially when he thought about their nearest relatives the termites. But they were almost as irksome as the flour beetles, and besides, he told himself, he couldn't stop the devils from launching their nuclear weapons. Foreknowledge did not equal culpability. And who listened to cockroaches anyway?

Crich settled more deeply into his prickly, yellow cushion of insulation and thought how if he woke up tomorrow and found himself king of the world, it would not be his fault at all. And when the others looked to him for answers, when they asked what had happened and how it all came to pass, he would explain that, regarding the devils' stewardship of the earth, mistakes had definitely been made.

And, when word came that the termites had perished—if pressed as to the timing of his knowledge and whether any attempt had been made to alert their relatives so they might seek shelter in the depths of the earth—Crich would try first to pass it off as fake news. His followers were loyal above all else so there was a good chance it would stick. But if that didn't work, he would just banish anyone who dared criticize him and assure everyone else he was doing a tremendous job, acknowledging that, in times such as these—in times of such unprecedented upheaval—mistakes may have been made, but certainly not by him.

❁

DISCUSSION QUESTIONS

1 How does Horace respond to the canines leaving the coalition? What does this reaction indicate about his leadership style?

2 What methods does Horace use to address dissent from the goats? What does this reveal about his approach to leadership?

3 How would you describe Horace's view of himself compared to the other animals? How does this view affect his leadership?

4 Why do the cows experience shame? What approach does Horace take to their shame?

5 Why do you think Crich decides not to warn the others?

6 How did the use of farm animals to portray political disputes affect you as a reader? Why might the author have chosen farm animals for this story?

7 Did this story make you feel more optimistic or pessimistic about contemporary democracies?

8 What aspects of the story seem liminal to you? (Consider setting, characters, and action.) Is there a liminal guide, and if so, what is the nature of their interaction with other characters?

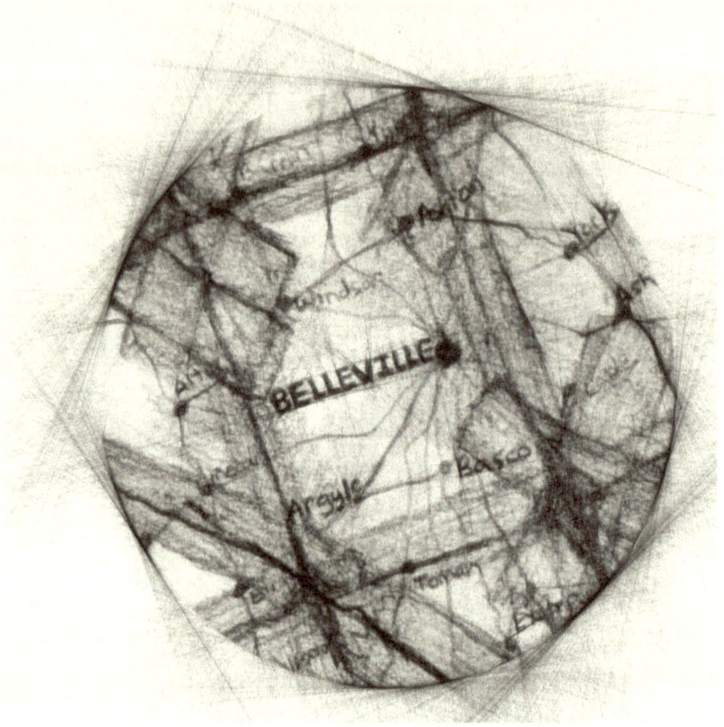

PRE-READING QUESTIONS

- Imagine a worst-case global warming scenario: Rising heat waves have displaced billions of people fleeing from coastal cities, brewed devastating storms, and evoked widespread famine. As refugee crises ignite geopolitical tensions and staggering inequality, widespread war makes it difficult to survive. When you consider that no single person's lifestyle change is likely to alter this outcome, what is your reaction?
- What was a moment–perhaps of failure or loss–where you felt powerless? How do you personally cope with tragedies you can't change?
- What do you think the world would be like without musicians, dancers, writers, singers, actors, filmmakers, and artists?
- If you're artistic, do you ever feel like your skills and talents aren't valued as much as other more practical skills and talents?

ALL HE COULD DO IS SING

TROUBADOUR JOE TRUDGED DOWN THE EMPTY HIGHWAY, his loafers scuffing up a peculiar array of brightly colored papers that littered the broken asphalt. He wondered where they came from. In decades past, he might have speculated a caravan of salespeople driving to afternoon appointments, oblivious of open briefcases forgotten on the top of their cars, promo sheets fluttering behind them on the wind. He knew of course that such a scenario under any circumstance was unlikely, just as he knew that now it was all but impossible. A yellow piece of paper stuck to the duct tape holding together his left shoe and a green piece stuck to the tape holding together his right, but he didn't mind. Such surprising splashes of color in the otherwise cold, gray world were like confetti at a funeral—welcome, cheerful accessories for the shoes he'd taken off a dead man a few towns back. He felt a little bad about it, but it was hard to find shoes his size. 18s. And he'd already been barefoot a couple of weeks. Months, maybe. The young man's legs and feet had been rigid like hockey sticks, but Troubadour Joe worked until he had them off, and then stayed despite the stench of decay, to sing the young man's passage. He always stayed, whatever the condition of the body, long enough for that. He couldn't bury every corpse he found—not at his age and with so little food to sustain him—and he consoled himself with the two-part reality of decomposition, which was that the flesh of the dead would be consumed whether above or below ground, and that every living thing needed to eat. What mattered, after all, was the passage.

That was weeks ago. He hadn't seen anyone since, dead or alive. It was like that though—long successions of silent, solitary days. In his early itinerant years, he would fall under the anxious spell of the uncanny quietude, but now he travelled in tranquil communion with the dying planet. It was morbid when you thought about it in one way, but not when you thought about it in another—the earth was in passage and he would sing it to rest. It was the least he could do. When he was young, he had wanted to save the world. He went to protests. Signed petitions. Stopped eating meat and driving cars. He'd even tried to run for office. But he'd been too late and too limited. Too insignificant and too ill-equipped.

"You're useless!" his distraught young wife had screamed one night, throwing cans of cream-style corn and then baked beans at him as the world bore full throttle toward its demise. She'd broken a glass punch bowl they'd received as a wedding gift on the wall just inches from his head. He had nothing to say in reply. He knew by then it was true. There were gifts people had. Skills they acquired. Traits and competencies that made them useful in an apocalypse, but he possessed none of them. All he could do is sing.

The next town came into view, nestled in a valley a mile off the highway. He pulled out his map, torn at the seams and fading from wear, and spread it on the hood of a deserted sedan. It didn't matter what the town had been called but he liked to know. He sang the towns too. Each of them had its own story. Its own life. Its own death. He traced his finger down the map.

Belleville.

He'd been in a Pleasantville, Ashville, Starkville, Haleyville, Shepherdsville, Evansville, Louisville, Rushville, Platteville, and Neillsville, but he'd never been in a Belleville.

Troubadour Joe folded up the map and put it back in his pack. Checked the car for food though he knew there would be none. Found a safety pin under a floor mat and used it to close a tear in his pack, then sat in the driver's seat for a while, resting his weary bones. He would sit for just a bit, long enough to sing the safety pin and the car and the person who had to abandon it there. Troubadour Joe turned the rearview mirror in his direction and smiled at the old man smiling back at him. He could feel the swell of another melody, this one for himself and, though it surprised him a little, he didn't question it because he never questioned the melodies—just gave himself over to them whenever he felt the valve open inside. So, Troubadour Joe sang. He sang his creased, black skin and his long white hair. He sang his old bones and his aching feet, he sang the miles he'd walked and the towns he'd helped pass, and he didn't stop until the tingling in his fingers went away and the valve inside him closed. It was a good singing, he thought, and a good rest, but now he best be on his way, for the world was passing away and he didn't want to leave any part of it unsung.

The papers continued all the way down the broad spiral of the off-ramp, narrowing to a single winding strip, like a trail of breadcrumbs. He smiled and followed them down into Belleville.

So many towns over so many years. In the early days of his itinerancy, a dread used to fall upon him whenever he approached a new town. He'd been terrified of the eaters. Every encounter with a new person or group had been a harrowing event, not knowing if he was being welcomed to their fireside for the sharing of his fellowship or the consuming of his flesh. But that all changed once he started singing them. Once he started doing that, whether they proved to be pilgrims or predators became irrelevant. It was true—he'd had to wrench open the valve at first—his terror having stuck it shut and stuck it shut good—but once he got it open, a melody more primal than the fear that threatened to paralyze his limbs would begin to flow. Like rusty water being pumped through the lines of an old well, the notes would start out on a scale tainted by this fear of the *Other*. But if he extended his hands and let it flow, soon those inharmonic notes would be flushed from his system, and new notes would emerge from a scale he'd never heard before. Vast and echoing, harmonizing yet distinct, the new melodies would open up inside him, and the song he sang would open up the world. What had previously been the most dreaded part of his travels was now the most cherished. It was his portal. His secret staircase. His key to the gates of a world subsisting within the one that he touched and felt, that he heard and smelled and saw.

Troubadour Joe paused at the end of the ramp. The papers followed the road to the right, which led into town. He wondered who had troubled themselves and why. So freshly laid with such deliberate placement, the path they made both intrigued and unsettled him. Whatever it meant, whatever it portended, it would become part of the singing. First step off the ramp, he began to hum. It always took a while to get to the heart of the song and, by the time he got to the heart of any town, he liked to be deep in the singing of it.

After a while, the trail of papers broke out into a hopscotch. Troubadour Joe grinned and hopped his way across, keeping balance with his staff. The path then resumed its single-line formation, and he continued down it smiling, but sometimes frowning. In all his years travelling the highways and the byways, he had never seen anything like it. He tried to figure what it meant, but there was a hum rising in his chest, urging him toward song. He attuned himself to its vibrations and let the strange notes take shape.

The road into town carved its wide heaving way past the same abandoned franchises that marked the entrance to every town he'd ever been through with a population once over six thousand. Gas stations, dollar stores and fast-food drive-thrus. There was even a pizza joint, but only the carryout kind. He sang them all.

Just before Main Street at the corner bank, Troubadour Joe paused. He could feel someone tugging at the melody. He looked for a bit, then saw her behind the drive-thru window. A middle-aged woman with straight black hair and sunken eyes stared out at him. When their eyes connected, she lifted her hand to the glass, and the melody turned and surged. Troubadour Joe spread his hands. He sang the woman and her sorrow. He sang her children and her home. He sang her regrets and joys and then, when there was nothing more to weave into the melody, he sang her passage.

When her image faded away and the song turned back to the trail, Troubadour Joe moved on. The river of color continued its curious course down Main Street, appearing to end at a clock tower in the center of the town square. The humming in his chest expanded as he went, and, after a bit, he opened his mouth to let it begin. Singing the passage of a town was always deep work. Its collective nature would at first evoke a layering of notes that rang out of him in disharmonies proportionate to the level of rancor that had existed in the community, but would eventually resolve in tranquil accord, letting him know its passage was complete. Oddly, no such discordant melodies emerged as he made his way down the rainbow road, only the sweet harmonies of resolution. Perhaps he had been mistaken. Perhaps he had been in Belleville before and had already sung its passage.

At last, he reached the town square and stopped beneath the clock tower. It was covered almost all the way to the top with the same blue, orange, red, green, yellow, and purple papers. A young girl of seven or eight with freckled skin and long, curly red hair stood toward the top of a tall ladder, gluing blue papers over the face of the clock. The hem of her green dress hung dirty and ragged a few inches above her bare feet.

"Welcome to Belleville, Troubadour Joe," the little girl called down to him. "I've been waiting for you."

Troubadour Joe was glad to know someone had been waiting for him. Never, in any of the thousands of towns that he'd been through, had anyone ever been waiting for him. He was deep in the singing of it though and wasn't sure he should stop to talk. But the melodies were so pure and bright, he wondered if it might be all right.

The little girl continued as though she understood. "It's okay." She smiled as she plastered a final orange sheet in the center of the blue ones to make a flower. "You can stop singing now."

Troubadour Joe cocked his head to the side and attuned himself to the sensations in his chest. It was true. The vibrations had settled. He let the song recede and, when it was resolved, he hollered up to the girl, "That sure is a pretty tower you're making."

"I'm so glad you think so," she beamed down at him, "because I made it for you!"

"Well, I'll be," he said. Never in all his years, in all his travels, had anyone ever decorated a tower for him.

"I've been working on it all morning," she said cheerfully and then stretched to add the last few pieces of yellow paper to the pediment.

"Did you leave that nice trail of papers for me too?" he asked.

"Yes, I did!" the little girl replied as she scooted down the ladder and stood in front of him, her green eyes sparkling. "Did you like the hopscotch?"

"Why yes," Troubadour Joe said with a smile, "I did."

"Did you hop it?" she asked, leaning in expectantly.

"Well, of course," Troubadour Joe replied.

The little girl squealed and clapped her hands. "I hoped you would!" She smiled at him for a bit, then added, "You know, you can take your pack off now and sit down. I'm sure you wouldn't mind a rest." She pointed at the park bench next to them. "Why don't you take off your shoes too," she suggested.

Troubadour Joe looked at the park bench and considered the girl's suggestion. He usually kept moving during the day. So much singing to do. And he'd already rested for a bit in the sedan. But it did sound nice. Taking off the pack. The shoes. Resting his weary bones.

"I suppose I could for a while ..." he replied as he slipped off his pack and sat down. Out of habit, he started humming. Priming the pump for whatever singing the little girl might need. He untied his left shoe and eased it off over his bunion, then untied the right one and forced it off over his swollen ankle.

"Do you always decorate like this?" he asked.

"Well," she explained, "I paint with whatever I can find. Sometimes it's actual paint. Sometimes it's old birthday plates or Solo cups. Sometimes it's plastic flamingos. This time, I found a whole closet full of paper sealed up tight in shrink wrap!"

"That must have been quite a sight," Troubadour Joe said with a smile.

The little girl nodded again. "I knew I would be painting a special passage this time."

"Oh," said Troubadour Joe, "so you're in the passage business too?" He felt a little confused but also pleasantly surprised.

"Oh yes," she said, "There's no other business I could be in."

"Why's that?" Troubadour Joe asked.

"Well," she shrugged and smiled, "all I can do is paint."

Troubadour Joe nodded. "That's how I ended up in the business. Except for me it was singing."

"I know," the little girl said, another bright smile breaking out across her face. "I could hear you coming a couple towns away."

"Well, isn't that something," Troubadour Joe said. She sure

was a sweet little girl and he thought he really ought to sing her, but it felt so good just to sit there and rest. To have his shoes off, to talk with her, to admire the clock tower she'd decorated just for him.

The little girl looked at him for a bit, then said kindly, "You don't have to sing the passages anymore, Troubadour Joe."

"Well, who will do it if I don't?" he asked. It troubled him to think of all the weary souls, living and dead, all the things, abandoned and decaying, the world itself, without the singing.

"There are others who can do it now, others who can sing and write and paint them, like me."

Again, Troubadour Joe felt troubled. He was glad to know there were others in the passage business, but he worried that if he stopped, some that needed singing might be missed.

The little girl set her hand on his. It was small and dirty and covered in dried paste. "When you've reached the world within the world, Troubadour Joe, you have *new* songs to sing."

"Is that where I am now?" he asked, sitting up and looking around. "I thought I was in Belleville." He looked at her, confused.

"This *is* the beautiful city, Troubadour Joe, the world within the world. *You made it*," she smiled, "and I painted your passage for you."

Troubadour Joe stared blankly at the little girl for a bit, then began to understand. He looked up at the tower, then back down at her.

"Was it the eaters? Did they get me at last?"

"No," she said, shaking her head and smiling gently. He could feel the rumblings of a hum coming on. "You hadn't eaten for quite a while, and, when you closed your eyes to rest in that old sedan up on the highway, you just never woke up."

"I see," Troubadour Joe nodded. "So, my body's up there, rotting?"

She replied, her eyes apologetic, "Like they all do."

"Well, you can't bury every corpse you find these days," he sighed, "not when you haven't eaten for a couple of weeks."

She bit her lip and shook her head. Troubadour Joe looked up at the tower.

"You painted this for my passage, eh?"

The little girl nodded and smiled. "And all the way back to the road!"

"Even better than a red carpet," he said.

The little girl's eyes grew wide. "Do you really think so?"

"I really, truly do."

The little girl beamed. The hum vibrating in his chest would not be put off any longer, so he gave leave to the valve to open up.

The girl's eyes grew even wider, and she whispered with rapt intensity, "You'll sing *new* songs now, Troubadour Joe. Songs you can't even imagine."

The humming grew louder, the valve almost all the way open now.

"That's right, Troubadour Joe," the little girl whispered, her eyes still wide, a gentle smile gracing her face. "Let the old songs go." Her green eyes twinkled. "Let the new ones come."

Troubadour Joe could feel everything he'd ever sung rise within him. All the trees and roads, all the people and towns, all the stories and passages he had ever sung swelled and folded into new harmonies that filled and lifted him right off the park bench.

"That's right, Troubadour Joe," the little girl called from below, her eyes wide and glistening, her smile happy and sad, full and true, "That's right!"

The notes surged and expanded, lifting him upwards along the rise of the clock tower. The vibrant hues of the last stretch of his passage danced with the notes emerging inside him. As he rose above the pediment of the clock tower, strange but marvelous new melodies of color and sound swelled to a tidal wave that busted apart the old valve within. Never in all his years had the melodies been this glorious. The notes so full of vibrations and light. As the music rushed toward his trembling lips, Troubadour Joe opened his mouth and let it flow, for all he could do is sing.

DISCUSSION QUESTIONS

1. What is happening to Troubadour Joe's planet? How did Troubadour Joe react to this situation as a young man?
2. How has Troubadour Joe's attitude toward the planet's imminent death changed as he's become older?
3. Why does Troubadour Joe's wife throw a punch bowl at him? Does Troubadour Joe agree with his wife's opinion of him or not? How does he cope with his lack of post-apocalyptic skills?
4. What does Troubadour Joe sing about for the towns he visits? What does the metaphor of the song as a "portal" or "secret staircase" suggest about his connection to the world outside himself?
5. Why do you think Troubadour Joe sings?
6. What do you think is meant by "the passage business?"
7. Why do you think Troubadour Joe is surprised to learn the little girl is in the passage business? Why do you think the little girl paints?
8. Troubadour Joe says that the girl's painting is "even better than a red carpet." What does this metaphor tell you about how he views the girl's work?
9. Why do you think the author included in the story a little girl who paints rather than just leaving the story about Troubadour Joe?
10. How does Troubadour Joe's life end? What would you like your own final moments in the world to look like?
11. What aspects of the story seem liminal to you? (Consider setting, characters, and action.) Is there a liminal guide, and if so, what is the nature of their interaction with other characters?

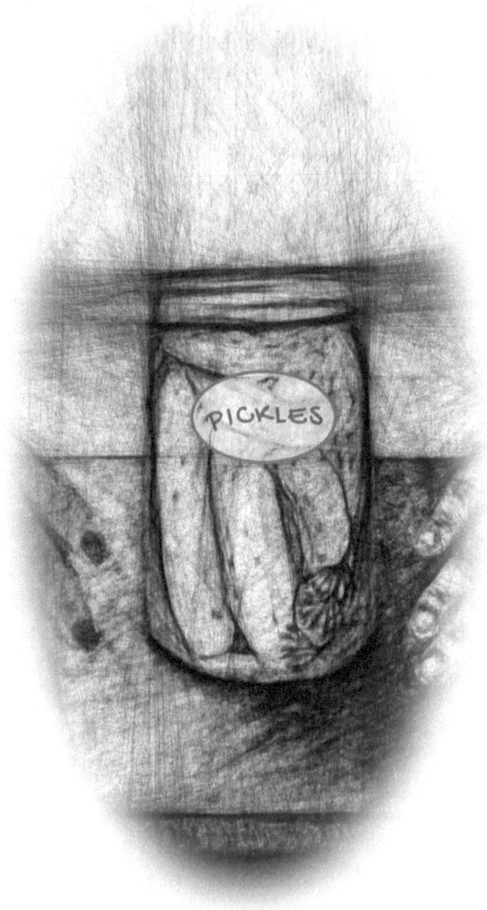

PRE-READING QUESTIONS

- Think of a recent argument where you strongly wanted to be right. Was your desire to be right beneficial or harmful?
- How did you feel about receiving advice from your parents while growing up? Were there any memorable phrases or sayings that had a lasting impact?

WHEN THEY COME FOR ME

WHEN THEY COME FOR ME, I WON'T GO DOWN without a fight. That's my solemn promise to you. Who do they think they are, anyway, having a say in everything there is to have a say about? It's a worldwide conspiracy and nobody's doing a damn thing about it. Whatever *they* say goes: *They* say you should only eat fish twice a week. Yeah? Well, it's free in the lake and I like to fish, so *fuck off. They* say you should drink eight glasses of water a day. Yeah? Well, I don't really want to spend all day pissing in the gutter, so *fuck off. They* say, if you believe there's some kind of worldwide conspiracy, you're a paranoid schizophrenic and you need help. Yeah? Well, of course they say that and pardon me if I'm repeating myself but *fuck off.*

They've been hunting me for decades, but up until now I've always kept one step ahead of them. They don't like keeping guys like me on the loose. I see things clearer than the average bloke, and that scares the hell out of them. The guys that are actually crazy? They let them wander around shouting nonsense, scaring pedestrians. They let them live in their tents under the bridge. Guys like me who can see what's really going on get rounded up and put away. They don't want us out here, pointing out the obvious. People should be able to see this all for themselves but for some reason they don't. People just go around spouting off all the propaganda they've been fed, quoting *they* without any understanding of what they're doing. My life's mission has been to wake people the fuck up. People get all worked up about the illuminati and the deep state, but what I've been saying for years to anybody who will listen is that it's *they* we have to worry about.

Last night, I holed up in an old warehouse downtown with a bunch of kids who were there to get high, kids who didn't understand the necessity of vigilance, kids who laughed when I told them they needed to be on their guard.

"How many times a week do you quote them?" I asked. "Or have them quoted to you? Start keeping track. Make a list of all the things you've heard directly attributed to *they*: *They* say you should save twenty percent of your income. *They* say you should change your oil every 3,000 miles. *They* say you should wear a condom, use LED light bulbs, stay in school, wash your hands, sleep on your left side, and never ever wear plaid with stripes."

"Yeah," a freckled kid in a T-shirt three sizes too big for him said. "They say all that shit."

"They do!" I nodded, excited that at least one of them was getting it. "But did you ever notice how they say you shouldn't judge a book by its cover, but they also say the clothes make the man? They say third time's a charm, but they also say three strikes and you're out. They say beware of Greeks bearing gifts, but they also say never look a gift horse in the mouth. I mean, what the hell is that all about?"

"It's bullshit," a pimple-faced boy with long, greasy hair cried. "They aren't even consistent!"

"Exactly!" I said, really, really excited and starting to pace. "They just pump this stuff out, shove it down your throat, and make you digest it over and over again until you don't even notice what they're spoon feeding you. Until you're zombies! Robots! Mindless automatons, marching to their beat, lapping up the milk straight from their teats, smiling as they jerk the strings of your pathetic puppet life!"

"Dude, that's kind of harsh," one of the big guys said. "And you need to calm the hell down."

"Look," I said, sitting down because I'd been told before it makes people nervous when I pace. "This is serious. You have no idea how many of their dictates you are following every single minute of your life. The ones you're aware of—the ones where *they* are actually cited as the source—those are just the tip of the iceberg. You don't even recognize how much *they* are in your head. The steady barrage of messages they've been sending to your subconscious from the time your mothers pushed you out of their nether parts."

"Gross," a girl with black lipstick and purple hair said.

"Like subliminal advertising," a chubby kid with a leather jacket piped in.

"Exactly!" I shouted, homing in on him and ignoring the girl. "They say it without saying it! If you buy this car, you'll be happy. If you own this phone, you'll be liked. If you use this shampoo, you'll be beautiful. It's the evil genius of it all! But once you get the revelation, you'll start to see it, just like I did, start to see how you've been living your entire life under their control!" I grabbed one of the young men by the sleeve, but he pushed my hand away. "They will never stop coming for you until their domination is complete! You must believe me when I tell you that your freedom will only come through knowledge, vigilance, and courage!"

I finished my sermon, dizzy from the heights of my illuminated sight. I looked at the kids, who were quiet and looking at each other. No one was laughing anymore. I thought maybe I'd gotten through to them, finally made them see, but then two of the biggest kids rushed at me and threw me out of the warehouse. I grabbed the biggest kid's leg and begged him to let me stay so that I might still try to show them the light, but he shoved me back on the ground. "You need to get the fuck outta here! They say you're crazy, man."

I sat there for a moment stunned. Never before had I had such a close call. If I had known—if I had understood how close *they* were! That they had already been around, spreading their lies about me to the very same kids I was trying to convince. If those kids hadn't warned me I could have been rounded up and strapped down, my brain electrified and reorganized, my synapses harangued and rearranged until I saw things the way *they* wanted me to see them. My only consolation in the whole fiasco was that it was confirmation that what I was doing was working. I was spreading the truth, and they were terrified.

I fled the city. All night long I ran, darting off the road into the woods or ditches or cornfields whenever I heard a car approaching. I am no stranger to pursuit. I've travelled back and forth across this shackled land, north and south, east and west, big towns, small towns, campgrounds and playgrounds, preaching deliverance from the almighty *they*. But I knew I was running out of places to go. Everywhere I went, they followed, taunting me, hunting me. I knew my days were numbered. I knew, one day soon, they would catch up with me.

When I got into town this morning, it was Sunday and church was just getting out. My nerves were shot and my head was pounding, but I didn't want to miss out on the opportunity. I stumbled up the courthouse steps just down the street from the church, launching my sermon with all the contradictory food advice they give because at least when it comes to that everybody already knows what I'm saying is true.

"They say," I began, weak and lightheaded from a lack of food, parched and pasty from a lack of water, and weary and confused from a lack of sleep, "coffee makes you gain weight and get cancer! But they also say it can help you lose weight and prevent cancer!"

A couple of the passersby glanced up, so I went on encouraged.

"They say soy is a miracle food, but they also say it's the devil's food. They glorify the potato out of one side of their mouths, but they vilify it out of the other."

No one stopped to listen. They were all just hurrying home to watch the game or heading to the corner cafe for brunch. I worried I was the problem. I wasn't finding my rhythm. Frazzled from my close call at the warehouse and exhausted from my midnight escape, I hadn't tapped into my higher sight and was just quoting facts.

I took a moment to scan the street to see if they had tracked me there. No sign of them yet. That was good. But people were just hurrying by, and I was losing precious time. Maybe I hadn't taken the right approach. Sometimes you had to invoke the authority of *they* to undermine it. It was a tricky business though—one I didn't like to engage in unless absolutely necessary.

I wiped my forehead and, trembling, raised my arms. "They

say ask and you shall receive. Seek and you shall find. Knock and the door shall be opened unto you, but they also say—"

"Excuse me, sir," someone interrupted. Finally, I got someone. An old woman, small and spry, white hair curled tight between her wrinkled brown forehead and her silk green hat. A matching green purse hung from the crook of her right elbow, and a small brown paper bag perched in the left.

She continued politely, "I just wanted to let you know you've got your attribution wrong on that one."

"What? I do?" I asked, all of a sudden confused and unsure of my entire approach.

"Mmm hmmm," she nodded. "The good Lord himself said that. But no worries. Next time just make sure you give credit where credit is due."

"Thank you, ma'am," I said, wondering how I could have made such an obvious mistake.

"Say, are you hungry?" she asked. "I've got a lunch I was going to share with my friend, Alvira, but she couldn't make it to church today on account of her grandchildren visiting."

I was hungry but, even more so, I was vigilant. I studied the bushes in the park across the street to see if maybe this lady was part of some scheme to trap me, because that's how they like to get you—rush at you when you aren't paying attention—but things looked clear, so I said, "Yes, ma'am. Thank you."

I expected her to hand me the lunch bag. That's what they usually do. Drop it at my feet or hold it out to me from a distance. But she came up the stairs, sat down beside me, and opened it.

"I hope you like egg salad," she said. "It's Alvira's favorite." She handed me one of the sandwiches.

"Egg salad is tasty," I agreed but felt that precaution dictated I test her. "They say that you shouldn't eat eggs ..."

She dismissed this with a wave of her hand. "But they also say you should eat them. I'm eighty-two, and I don't really pay attention to all that anymore."

"Respect," I said and meant it. I took a huge bite of the sandwich and stared at her.

"You like sweet pickles?" she asked. "I made them myself." She opened a mason jar and held it out to me. I was about to reach for one, but then she smiled and I froze. What if she was a trap? A clever, clever trap they sent to lure me into eating a poison pickle. But were they out to kill me or repurpose me? I always wanted to know. Neither was a great option, but I would die before I let them turn me into one of their pawns.

"You first," I said, eyeing her sideways.

"Okay," she said, "they're here if you want them." She set the jar between us, then took a pickle out and started munching on it. Something moved in the bushes across the street. I stood up to see, knocking over the pickle jar.

"Oh ... I'm sorry," I said, setting the jar aright and brushing the juice from the step, all the while keeping an eye on the bushes.

"What are you looking for?" she asked, blotting at the pickle juice that soaked into her skirt with a napkin.

"Nothing," I lied. "I just thought I saw someone."

"Are you expecting somebody?"

"Sort of. And, if they come, I might need to make a run for it. If I don't get to say thank you or goodbye, I do apologize in advance."

"I don't think you've got anything to worry about," she said. "Just try to enjoy the sunshine and the sandwiches and, after we finish, I've got chocolate chip cookies we can share."

A chocolate chip cookie sounded pretty good. I shoved the rest of the sandwich in my mouth and was really enjoying it until I started wondering where all this supposed hospitality was coming from.

"You know," I said, some of the egg salad flying out of my mouth onto her dress as I talked, "they say you shouldn't talk to strangers."

"It's true," she replied, "They do say that."

"But you don't listen to them ..."

She shrugged. "I guess I like to make my own decisions."

She handed me a cookie and started eating one herself. I really, really wanted it, but it was possible that there was poison in my cookie and not in hers.

"Did you really make these for your friend Alvira, or are you just saying that?" I asked, all of a sudden very upset. I grabbed hold of her wrist, and she dropped her cookie. "Is Alvira an actual person or just some goddam front they're using to get control over me?"

Her eyes grew wide, and she leaned back beneath my penetrating glare. "She's real ..." she stammered. I could feel her arm trembling in my grip. I could see the fear in her eyes. Her voice, though it quavered, had notes of kindness and sincerity.

I closed my eyes to sort it out, my grip like iron around her wrist. I wanted to believe her. I almost believed her. But then I heard something move again in the bushes across the street, and my head jerked in that direction.

My eyes jumped back and forth, blinking and glazed, from bush to bush and bench to bench, then scanned the buildings and sidewalks beyond. That's when she touched my arm and said, "Sir, you know they've got help for people like you ..."

My gaze slowly returned to her, and I stared, stunned at her brazen confession. A look passed over her face—a realization of what she had just said. The slip of her tongue. And that's when it happened. My free hand reached for the jar of pickles and brought it down on her head. The jar broke, and she went limp. The pickles spilled onto the stairs, and I was left clutching a large shard of glass, which sliced open my hand. Blood dripped from my clenched palm, but I held her fast. They could have trained her to fake it, and I couldn't take any chances. I brought the shard down into her neck, then released her wrist. She slumped back. Her blood oozed out onto the courthouse steps, mingling with my own.

Someone screamed and I ran. I fled through the streets of the town, past the ignorant, blind masses gorging themselves on pancakes and bacon and the endless stream of indoctrination pouring out of their phones and televisions, preparing them, like calves fattened for the slaughter, for the coming of *they*. I could hear their footsteps behind me. I knew this was the day. They yelled after me, but I didn't listen. They commanded me to stop, but I ran anyway. They shot at me, but I kept going. I kept going and going, and now I'm here, in the river, hiding like a rat, shivering and bleeding in the mud but comforted by the knowledge that I have spent my life in the service of your liberation. I can hear the sirens. I can hear the dogs. I know they are coming. I know this time I won't get away, but I will never ever let them take me. And I swear to you, I won't go down without a fight.

DISCUSSION QUESTIONS

1 The narrator rejects conventional wisdom about drinking water. Does this reaction make you sympathize with the narrator more or less?

2 Consider the contradiction between "the clothes make the man" and "never judge a book by its cover." How does the narrator feel about these sayings? Do you think these types of sayings can be useful or not?

3 What strategies does the narrator use to capture the teenagers' attention?

4 Why do you think people experience anger when leaders appear contradictory, especially during crises like a pandemic?

5 Do you believe that people today trust common-sense wisdom too much or too little, given the current social and political climate?

6 What specific topic ignites the narrator's passion? How does his message resemble a "sermon" rather than casual speech?

7 The narrator claims to see from the "heights" of his "illuminated sight." What does this spatial metaphor say about how he views himself?

8 In what ways does the old woman connect with the narrator?

9 What does it indicate about the narrator's mindset that he interprets the old woman's offer of help as "brazen" and a "confession"?

10 How could a compassionate offer from an elderly woman ('Sir, you know they've got help for people like you...') provoke such a violent reaction in the narrator?

11 When speaking with the old woman, the narrator says: "They say you shouldn't talk to strangers..." Do you think this story reinforces or questions that message?

12 What does the narrator believe at the end of his life? What's wrong with wanting to be free and think independently?

13 The narrator is comforted by the knowledge that he has "spent his life in the service of your liberation." How might believing that you don't only stand for your own desires–but that you serve a bigger cause–actually make a person more destructive?

14 What aspects of the story seem liminal to you? (Consider setting, characters, and action.) Is there a liminal guide, and if so, what is the nature of their interaction with other characters?

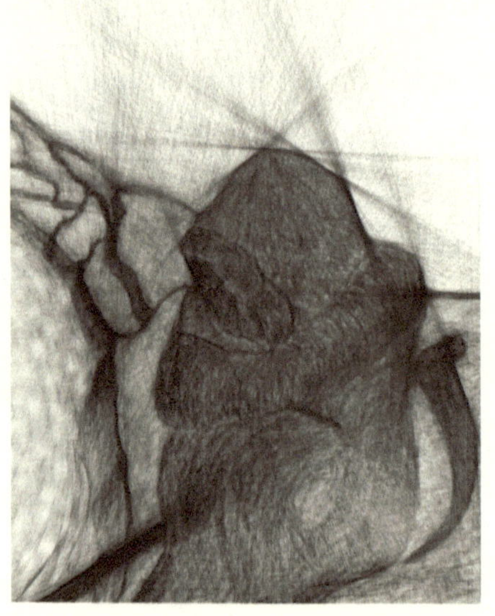

PRE-READING QUESTIONS

- How do you feel about spending time with people who are near death? Why do you think some people voluntarily choose this as their profession?
- In the United States, people live longer than ever, but many spend the last part of their lives with chronic conditions requiring restrictive treatments in hospitals or nursing homes. If you learned you had a terminal condition, how would you want to spend your final days?

THE FERRYMAN AND HIS BROTHER

HE'S MY BROTHER, BUT HE NEVER LETS ANYONE KNOW it. Since it doesn't make much difference for most of the passengers, I don't usually bother to clarify. They've got enough on their minds. Regrets and whatnot. If they've got a lot of them, their crossing will take a long time, and if I distract them with irrelevant matters it might take even longer, so I just let them do what they need to do in peace and quiet, and I focus on getting them safely to the other side.

I take a different approach though when one of the imperious types comes aboard, humbled not even by the circumstances that brought them to me. In these cases, I make sure they know. Of course, my brother can't do anything more to them, and on some level they know that, but there's still psychological resonance from their recent experience with him, and, because his personage has reigned so mythically over their lives, just letting them know we're related is usually enough to silence their demands, lower their chins, and put them in the frame of mind they ought to be in, lest their crossing drag on needlessly. My brother says I don't have to do this. Argues that I shouldn't. Says it's not my place to remediate their suffering. He might be right. But I don't do it just for them. I do it for me too. I do not look forward to dreary, drawn-out trips across the river.

I never tell the children, of course. They're already a little frightened. Not entirely sure what's happening. They look up at me with searching, innocent eyes, hoping I'll explain things to them. As I said, I'm just supposed to ferry them, but for the littlest ones—even though the trip will be short, luminous, and immediately revelatory—I tell them they're about to embark on the greatest adventure of their lives.

Again, my brother doesn't approve. But I don't approve of some of his methods either. We used to fight all the time over how each of us ought to do our jobs but that was eons ago. Now we mostly just let each other do our jobs the way we see fit, though there are some lingering grudges and disputes.

For example, over half of everyone who comes to me brings some sort of payment, but I've never taken bribes and I never will. Somehow, though, this myth persists. I suspect my brother perpetuates it. His gothic tendencies have never abated. He says it's the job, but I know he relishes the art and poetry devoted to us—well, mostly to *him*—and he likes to keep the ancient stories fresh.

Since I have no practical use for the coins, I throw them into the river. There are hundreds of millions by now. Probably billions. No sunlight ever makes it down here to the underworld, of course, but some of the passengers shine so bright that, on their crossings, it looks like we're floating on a river of silver and gold. Unfortunately, those luminescent trips are the shortest but, even so, it's gratifying to collaborate in some small way in the creation of such radiant beauty, however fleeting, and to offer this small gift—a little something special from the ferryman—to the ones who shone brightest up top.

Passengers try to bribe my brother too. He takes their payoffs but only in cases where he wasn't really coming for them. He has no real say, after all, in the time he is to collect them. I've told him thousands of times it isn't fair to take bribes, but he claims it puts some of the pre-passengers at ease.

My brother can't stand it when pre-passengers try to cheat him though. He claims no one has ever succeeded. I think he's probably right, but I could never stand it when he gloated over it. For millennia, he enjoyed recounting the fates of Sisyphus and Gilgamesh and, for a while, all he could talk about was Count Dracula. I'm sure he would get a lot of laughs out of the billions of dollars pre-passengers spend on vitamins and herbal supplements these days, if the last century hadn't so thoroughly destroyed his joie de vivre.

Yes. I'm afraid it's true. The work has worn him down. You

would think the years would have made him indifferent, but they haven't. My brother has become cynical. Quite possibly, is going mad. From the very beginning, he had trouble with the killings—with all the ways there were for humans to die in the natural course of things, he couldn't fathom why they actively added to the means and ways of death by killing one another. I'm never up there in the world so I can't imagine what it would be like to witness that day in and day out, millennium after millennium, but, I tell you, it has changed my brother. He used to be so full of life—no bad puns intended—eager to be up there and part of it all—to see and discover, to watch as it all evolved. It was, in fact, the very reason he fought me for it.

As the older brother, it was supposed to be *my* job, but he wanted it so badly. For over a century, we wrestled for it, but, being equal in strength, neither of us could prevail. At first, I fought him on the principle of it. I was the older brother, and it was my right to take the best job, up in the world where everything was happening. But after a couple of decades of grappling and sweating, of takedowns and reversals, of tearing our way through the underworld, I began to wonder if I might not like it better down here, where the water ripples meditatively along the riverbank, where the drama of existence is already spent and only its echoes are ever heard. Eventually, I decided to stop fighting him for it, and we took up our respective roles. I still remember how he smirked as he donned the cloak and took the scythe from me, convinced he had secured for himself the better part.

But the last century almost did him in. He was so overworked at some points, I thought the exhaustion alone might overcome him. The real problem, though, was the killing—killing on a scale he'd never seen before. And, of course, my brother has seen everything.

It was during the first Great War when I first noticed the change. He developed an alarming sarcasm and would make caustic remarks, sometimes mocking the passengers, sometimes mocking the work. During the Great Purge, he became depressed and didn't say much of anything at all. Then the Second Great War hit. That's when I first began to fear my brother was going mad.

He started hanging around the dock after making a drop, shouting absurdities that both confused and terrified the passengers as I ferried them across the water. It was always something along the lines of, "You know it's because the gods are jealous of me! That's why they gave you the sweet ferryman gig and me the job of trash collector! You're no threat to them! Don't you see, brother, the gods fear me! They're trying to crush my spirit with the corruption of humanity! Eviscerate me with their villainy and vice!"

Sometimes, when we'd still be on the dock preparing to embark, he'd seize a passenger who'd taken the life of another, pull them close to his terrible face and, snarling and smirking, say things like, "When you get out into the middle of the river, where the fog is thickest and the water darkest, my brother's going to dump your waste of a life overboard and let you drown in the cold, murky waters of Old Styx—*eternally*." To avoid a scene, I would wait until we departed and then assure the threatened passenger that everyone was due a crossing, no matter how long it took, no matter how undeserving they might be.

During the Great Leap Forward, things really began to deteriorate. My brother took to pacing the riverbank when he knew that he was needed immediately and in multiple locations up top. He would sometimes shout, sometimes mumble, but would always repeat the same phrase, "It's only a matter of time ... it's only a matter of time ..."

"Until what?" one of the passengers once dared to ask.

"Until the next great war!" my brother roared, scythe raised, arms of his cape flailing in the wind, his crazed, yellow eyes flashing forth from his hood.

I understand his struggle. I'm not indifferent to the horrors. I feel bad for my brother. I feel bad for the passengers. In fact, the less the passengers glow, the worse I feel for them. What thoughtless, petty, or blatant shades of selfishness these dim vessels must have daily indulged in to arrive in such a state of ashen shadow. To have lived a life with such little light! It is unfathomable to me, down here guiding this ferry through the interminable twilight that hovers over Old Styx, that passengers would not have generated every bit of light they could while they still had the chance.

The long, gloomy crossings are not the worst part of the job, however. Sometimes, I get a black hole. A passenger who sucks in even the dim gray light of the netherworld, turning the journey across the river into a harrowing, unremitting night of impenetrable darkness. It's those times I wish I hadn't given my brother the job up top. I suppose I don't really know, though, whose job is more trying. I don't really know what it's like for him. I've never had to stand by and witness the genocide of entire peoples, simply there to collect the dead, powerless to stop the slaughter. But he doesn't really know what it's like for me either. To be held captive for endless ages to the moans and cries, to the teeth-gnashings and wormlike writhings of these black holes that perpetrate such dark deeds. He has no idea the toll these passengers take on me—he is too consumed with his own experience of them.

"You have no idea what I went through to get this one down here!" my brother once cried toward the end of the Second Great War as he shoved a passenger onto the jagged rocks at the dock. Without even looking, I could tell it was one of the black holes. I could feel the cold emptiness curling in on itself. Its power to devour just beginning its long, painful dissolution. My brother grabbed me by the shoulders.

"Millions, brother ... millions and *millions* ..." he whispered. I could feel his hands trembling. Could see his wild eyes in the depths of his hood. "All the way down here, they just kept appearing—crying out—reaching for us—accosting us—and they blamed *me*, brother—*me*—right along with *him*! How could they think it was *me*!"

I looked down at the murderous dictator lying at my feet and shuddered at the passage that awaited me. I tried to assure my brother, "They're just scared and confused—he's killed so many so fast. They just need you to pick them up and bring them to their rest. Once they get to the river, they'll begin to find peace. They will understand your role."

He began to shout, "I can't do it! I can't go back up there and bring them all down here. I can't do it." Then he raised the scythe over his head and hissed at the man at his feet, "I won't!"

"He's already dead," I reminded him, but he brought the scythe down anyway, slashing it, over and over again, through the passenger's vast emptiness, until at last my brother was spent and the scythe hung limp at his side.

I laid my hand on his shoulder. "They're waiting for you, brother," I reminded him as the passenger writhed on the ground with haunting, echoing moans. "You have an important job to do—perhaps the most important job in the whole world—even if you're misunderstood and unappreciated sometimes. You must go and do your work, brother."

He sighed but then, after a bit, headed back to the passengers waiting for him up top.

That was possibly the longest trip across the river I've ever experienced. I can't say for sure—there are a few others in the running. But when they're bleak and protracted like that for a passenger, they're bleak and protracted for me. In those long, tormenting trips, I lose track of time. I lose track of everything. Of myself. My purpose. The meaning of it all. Of meaning itself. The wailing and gnashing of teeth become my only reality, and I must reach deep into the recesses of my being and try to recall the light. Sometimes, I can only conjure up a solitary coin sparkling in the light of some gentle soul. But I hold onto it. Fixate on this single point of light holding out against the darkness. I make it my North Star, and I find my way through. I tried again today to explain this to my brother.

"You have to find the light!" He was having a particularly bad morning and was sitting on the bank, rocking back and forth, hands over his face, scythe sinking in the river. I reminded him about the coins and how the passengers who burn bright make the river sparkle. "You must think of things like this that you can hold onto when it's all too much. Surely, there are such things that you witness in your side of the work?"

He said nothing at first, just kept rocking and emitting long, quiet moans. Finally, after further encouragement, he offered half-heartedly, "Well, sometimes, there are passengers who give up their lives for others—remember that guy last week from Tabuk?"

"Yes!" I said. "He made Old Styx sparkle like a river of diamonds! That's good, brother, that's really good!" After more prodding, he conceded that there were often other things at the end, too. Kindnesses. Reconciliations. Acceptance.

"You must focus on *every* ray of light, brother, no matter how small," I enjoined him.

He nodded, but I'm not sure he was convinced. I wish I could have just let him sit there on the riverbank—sat there with him as brothers, side-by-side, in a much-needed respite, but we didn't have the time. The longer we sat, the more the passengers piled up for the both of us. I pulled his scythe from the river and got him to his feet.

"You must be strong, brother," I said, gripping his arms tight, "and you must always remember to look for the light!" He nodded, and though he couldn't quite raise his eyes to mine, he turned and headed back up toward the ridge.

As I got back onto the ferry and took up my pole, I looked over my shoulder at my brother, trudging up the rugged terrain to go collect his next passenger. I hoped for his sake it would be a glower. I hoped for his sake it wouldn't be a child gunned down in some senseless murder, but a benevolent elder, dying in old age, surrounded by her children and grandchildren, with songs and prayers and a thousand kindnesses. I hoped he wouldn't have to search for the light. I hoped it would be everywhere, in everyone and everything, and he could bathe in it for even just a little while. Let it fill him and renew him and give him strength for another day. Another decade. Another millennium. I hoped for my brother that the next passenger wouldn't be just a glower, but a *supernova*—an explosion of light that could override a thousand manifestations of desolation with just one glimpse of it. I hoped it for him. I hoped it for the world. And as I looked at my next passenger—grim and gray with only the feeblest emanation of light foretelling a bitter crossing through unrelenting gloom—I hoped it for myself.

DISCUSSION QUESTIONS

1 The ferryman tells his passengers that transitioning from life will be "short, luminous, and immediately revelatory—the greatest adventure of their lives." In what way could transitioning from life to death be "revelatory?" How might it seem like an adventure?

2 Why does the ferryman remind passengers that he is the brother of Death?

3 The ferryman believes that an "imperious" attitude is not the right frame of mind when transitioning from life to death. Why might he think this?

4 Why does the ferryman end up deciding to take his job?

5 What does the ferryman do with the coins he receives as payment for his services? What does that tell you about his approach to death?

6 The ferryman says that some passengers shine brightly in their transition. What kind of life do you personally think would shine brighter in the transition? What kind of life do you think would be pale and ashen in the transition?

7 What speech does the ferryman's brother occasionally give to the killers he escorts to the River Styx? How does the ferryman's brother's attitude toward his job change during the 20th century? Why do you think his attitude changes? What does the ferryman say to passengers after his brother has yelled at them? Do you agree with this philosophy?

8 What makes Death want to quit his job? If everyone is going to die, why do you think people sometimes turn to fear, anger, and blame when someone dies?

9 How does the ferryman encourage his brother when he feels like giving up? Why do you think he hopes to see an illuminated soul for himself? What emotional need is he trying to meet?

10 What aspects of the story seem liminal to you? (Consider setting, characters, and action.) Is there a liminal guide, and if so, what is the nature of their interaction with other characters?

PRE-READING QUESTIONS

- Do you think it's helpful or strange to live your life with no regrets?
- Would you like to be thought of as weird? Why?
- Do you think it's ever too late for people to change? Why or why not?

SHE SAW GERTRUDE STEIN IN THE CONDENSATION ON HER WINDOW

I DO MY SCOUTING FOR WOMEN THE OLD-FASHIONED WAY. At a bar. None of this app crap for me. Sure, it limits the dating pool, but I like it that way. Human interaction. First impressions. You just gotta be careful though. Lotta crazies out there. I might have actually met one a couple of months ago. Still ain't sure. I'd spent the day helping my buddy Paul drywall his basement and stopped in for a drink at Jenks'—an establishment downtown between the True Value and the bowling alley, where the locals hang out. See, I haven't been too keen on going home as of late. My wife left me beginning of the year and our only kid is all grown-up and working in Albania with the Peace Corps.

So there I am at Jenks' ordering a beer when this woman I never seen before walks in. She's the general age of a customer at Jenks'—fifty something—but you can tell she ain't from the neighborhood. Maybe the suburbs. Maybe out-of-towner. She's tall and thin, with a bony face and pretty, blue eyes, long, light brown hair, probably dyed. She's wearing makeup but it ain't caked on or nothing. Her clothes ain't quite right for Jenks'—it's all jeans and tank tops in here on a Saturday night—and she's got on this flowing blue dress and sandals. Her toenails ain't painted. Her fingernails neither. She sits down at the bar just a couple of empty seats away from me and orders a margarita.

The bartender sets her drink down, and she starts digging around in her oversized bag.

"Let me get that," I say.

"Oh ..." she says, looking unsure. "No, that's all right. I've got my wallet in here somewhere." She continues to dig, but I throw a ten on the bar. She looks at it and bites her lip. The bartender swipes it up before she can protest again.

"Thank you ..." she says, still a little unsure, then takes a long sip of her drink.

We make small talk about the weather and the bar. I tell her my name is Rick. She tells me hers is Seraphina. She drinks her first margarita down pretty quick, then orders another and asks me what I'll have. I'm thinking this is a good sign, but she insists on paying and explains it's cuz she don't know the rules no more, and that she's worried if she accepts a second drink from a man it means she's agreeing to sleep with him.

Course it's what I'm hoping for, but I don't wanna make her uncomfortable, so I just say, "Don't go out much?"

"No ... never, really," she replies, "I'm here for the opening of an exhibit tomorrow at the college and ... I didn't want to spend the whole night in my hotel room." *Mmm. Hotel room*, I'm thinking, *this is a good sign*. She puts her lips around the straw, and I try not to look at her mouth.

"It was considerate of you though," I say, "to let me know you don't wanna spend the night with me in case I wanna spend my money on another lady who might be more interested."

"Oh, yes, of course ..." she says, like she's apologizing, "Please feel free to go mingle—I realize these things take time."

"You'd be surprised," I say with a laugh. "But don't worry about it. I would enjoy conversing with you for a while," and then I add, "even if you don't wanna sleep with me." I mean it in a nice way, of course, and I'm pretty sure she gets that, but then her forehead gets all wrinkled up like she's worried about something, so I say, "What's the matter?"

She slurps on her margarita some more, then says, "It's just that ... I can tell you're too much of a gentlemen to have any *expectations*, but just in case you have any lingering *hopes* that our conversation might lead to something more, I think I should tell you now, in case you still want to cut your losses that, well, I'm not exactly ..." she looks around the bar, leans in real close and whispers, "*normal*."

Now, I seen some weirdos in my day. Crazies too. She don't

look nothing like any of them. She don't smell nothing like any of them. In fact, she smells pretty damn good. I pull my stool closer and ask her to explain. She takes a few more sips of her drink, then turns toward me with this real serious face.

"Well," she begins kind of nervous, "first of all, I'm what they call a *SLIder*, someone who experiences, or maybe causes, Street Light Interference. When I'm walking across a parking lot or down a sidewalk at night, a streetlight will sometimes just go out suddenly. One time, when I was in Trader Joe's, I stepped into an aisle and the whole row of lights went out, just like that. My son says the slider business is not an actual condition, just a function of confirmation bias, but that's his explanation for everything since he started college. You can bet I haven't told him about the *faces*."

I wasn't sure what confirmation bias was, but ever since my daughter went to college all she talks about is *implicit bias*, pointing out how we only got white guys on our construction crews around here. I told her we ain't sexist or racist, but she says it's deep down in our subconscious.

"What faces?" I ask.

"Well ... I *see* them. Like a woman with long hair in the bark of a tree or a pig with glasses in the embers of a fire. It's a condition called *pareidolia*."

"That's a *condition*?"

She nods, all serious, then takes another drink before going on. "And sometimes when the air conditioning is running at night, I hear voices or music, and, apparently, this is also considered an aspect of pareidolia, which used to be considered a precursor to psychosis but recently has been downgraded to a correlative of neurosis."

"Well, that don't sound too bad neither," I say, trying to think if I'd ever seen a face in a tree or heard a voice in the air conditioner, but for some reason the only thing in my head is the face of my old buddy Trevon from the army.

Seraphina goes on, a little emotional, the tequila starting to hit I suppose, "I mean, in days gone by, some people who saw faces and heard voices were considered prophets. The oracle of Delphi. Teresa of Avila. Today, these people are just pumped full of medication and put under psychiatric care. And what I want to know, Rick, is who drew the line between imaginative and neurotic? Between mystic and schizophrenic? Between genius and madness?"

"Prolly a bunch of schmucks who consider themselves normal."

"Yes ... that's got to be it," she says, putting her hand on mine. Her skin's a little wrinkled but soft. She's got crow's feet too, but everybody does at Jenks'. She sighs. "Why do you suppose we all value normalcy so much? I mean I understand from a Darwinian perspective that it's advantageous but how much of human life and potential are wasted, Rick, trying to make sure we fit in?"

I don't know what to say cuz I'm distracted. I'm sitting there with a beautiful woman having an intelligent conversation and a couple of drinks, but all I can think about is the last time I saw Trevon Williams. We were just outta the army, and I'd taken a job as a framer with my uncle. Trevon knew he was looking for another guy for his crew and asked me to put in a word for him.

Seraphina goes on, slurring her words a little as she talks, clearly not too used to drinking a whole lot. "I participated for decades in rituals that confirmed my normalcy—I attended Pampered Chef parties, made small talk at school events, drove a minivan, shopped the Vera Wang line at Kohl's—but I always felt like an imposter. I'm middle-aged now. My children are grown and flourishing. They don't even live near me anymore. There's no longer any risk to them if I don't fit in. If I want to swim naked in a creek or make my own dresses out of recycled silk scarves, why wouldn't I?"

I ain't gonna lie. I got hung up for a second on the swimming naked in the creek part, but I put it outta my mind. I was trying to be a better listener, cuz according to my ex it wasn't exactly a strong suit of mine.

Seraphina continues, "When my son found out that I stopped wearing a bra, he said, 'Next thing you know, you'll be joining up with the hippies, Mom.' *But*, I said to him, *I've always hated bras*. And then he said, 'But you always wore them.' And then I said, *Yes, but isn't that crazy?*"

Again, she had a point, but, again, I'm hung up on the fact that she ain't wearing a bra. I take a quick sideways look, but it's too hard to make anything out with the dress she's got on.

"I would never join up with the hippies," she says, shaking her head hard.

"Hell no," I say, shaking mine too.

"I mean I'm sure they're lovely people out there doing their best to live their dream with their camper vans and their beaded curtains and their herbal remedies, but they're just like any other group trying to live free from the hegemony of societal expectations—most of them just end up looking and acting and thinking *exactly* like everybody else in their group—and it's true whether the group is social or religious or political—it's even true for the *anarchists*!"

This last part about the anarchists seems to upset her the most. She takes hold of my shirt and pulls me in close. "The urge to conform is as strong as the nuclear force, Rick—its dictates as unconscious as the strong force on a quark."

She pushes me back, eyebrows raised, giving it all time to sink in I suppose, then adds, "At least quarks can't deceive themselves about what they're doing. Well, maybe they can. I guess we really don't know. How could we? We're all bumbling around here in Newton's realm, while they're all zipping around there in the quantum."

I'm really trying to pay attention, but again, for some reason, my mind keeps going back to Trevon. This time to the last conversation I ever had with him. My uncle told me he didn't need no more framers, and I had to go tell him.

I finish off my beer and say, "It's hard to be different. And it's hard to do things different than everybody else around you." She nods real pronounced, then finishes off her drink. "But you don't gotta worry about none of that other stuff, Seraphina. I'm telling you—you don't seem that strange."

"Well..." she says, pausing to order me another beer and herself another margarita, "that's very kind of you, Rick, but I haven't told you the half of it. I have dreams, too. Significant dreams in periods preceding significant changes in my life. Last week, just before waking, I was flying, like a bird, high above the ocean, all the way to Greece. It was a big deal because I'd *never* flown in a dream before. See, my husband—may he rest in peace—always had flying dreams. Sometimes he'd fly so high he'd lose control and start careening toward the ground, waking up just before he crashed. That was him though. Always taking chances, always pushing the limits. Sometimes, his risk-taking was too much for me, but I was always jealous of his flying dreams. The only way I could get anywhere fast in my dreams was by scooting along the ground, lying on some kind of invisible roller sled, pushing myself forward with my hands. And when I came across some obstacle, like a felled tree, I would have to stop. I knew what that difference in our dreams meant."

I feel sorta bad for her, you know, scooting around on the ground in her dreams while her husband's flying all over the place, so I say, "Eh ... they're just dreams."

"That's what my daughter says!" She laughs hard then, but it turns into a frown. She drinks down half her new margarita and says, "Did you know, Rick, that in days gone by, and in some isolated pockets still, those who have dreams and those who can interpret them are valued members of the community? Nowadays, if you know what your dreams mean, you're just a lonely, middle-aged woman on her way to owning thirteen cats and showing up downtown every lunch hour to play "Comfortably Numb" on a melodica in front of Starbucks!"

She starts crying and puts her head on my shoulder. Her hair is soft and smells like coconut. I don't say nothing, just put my arms around her and hold her nice against me. The truth is I have dreams too. Dreams you might call *significant.* A few of them about Trevon. But I don't pay no attention to them. In fact, I do my best to forget about them.

"I'm tellin' you, Seraphina, nothin' about you seems too weird."

"My daughter doesn't think so," she sniffs. "She called from Germany last week to give me her monthly pitch to join a book club or a Pilates class, but I've never really liked that sort of group thing, and I said what I always do, 'Thank you for the pep talk,' and she said, 'it's not a pep talk, Mom, *it's an intervention.*' And I guess what I really want to know is what's so wrong with seeing Gertrude Stein in the condensation on my window?" She pulls away from me but grabs me by the shirt again and pulls my face right up close to hers, "I mean the numinous can jump out at you from *anywhere.* It's not bound the way we are by social convention or the way quarks are by the strong force—it *is* the strong force, metaphorically speaking—though, perhaps, *literally* as well, we simply don't know—and it can commandeer any object for its purpose!"

"You saw Gertrude Stein in the condensation on your window?" I ask.

She releases my shirt and nods with an "I told you so" kind of look on her face.

"When?"

She sighs. "When I was trying to decide if I should go back to school to get an M.F.A."

"Ah," I say, like that explains everything. But the truth is I'm in a little over my head and a little too drunk to track what's going on in the conversation. I'm trying though, you know, cuz I ain't an asshole, and, yeah, I want to sleep with her, but I feel like we're connecting, you know, and that don't happen too often in this life, so I'm serious when I say I'm like actually trying to understand. "So, what you're sayin'," I say, "is that the strong force was in the condensation on your window."

"Maybe. I don't know—and I said the *numinous,* which may or may not be the same as the strong force." She picks up her margarita, unsteady, and sighs. "If I were twenty years younger, I'd go back to school and get a Ph.D. in physics to try and figure it out."

"Okay, but you're sayin' you think this *numinous* put Gertrude Stein on your window."

I pick up my beer as she sets down her margarita. She sloshes half of it on the bar and sways on her stool. "No ... I'm saying the numinous makes use of what's available. It breaks through the five walls of the senses to speak things to us in the silent, mysterious language of the soul."

I'm still trying to follow but to make things even harder, I'm getting this bad feeling in my gut and it just keeps growing. It ain't the beer neither. It's Trevon Williams back in my head. After he moved to Burlington and took that job as a janitor at the plastics factory, I thought I saw him around town like ten different times. But it wasn't ever him. He was my friend, you know, so I should have been disappointed, but I was always just relieved cuz I didn't know if I could look him in the eye, knowing my uncle hired another guy a few weeks later.

Seraphina slurps out the bottom of her glass with her straw, then closes her eyes and tips back her head as she continues, "*Apparently*, though, this is considered a *condition* as well. When you mistakenly perceive connections between unrelated things, it's called *apophenia*, which is considered far more serious than pareidolia, since pareidolia has been downgraded to a correlative of neurosis and apophenia is holding steady as a precursor to schizophrenia."

"Schizophrenia?" Well, now that did sound serious. I like her and everything, but, geez, I'm thinking, maybe she *is* a little crazy. I mean, Gertrude Stein? Who the hell is that anyway? I'm too drunk to sort it out, and I don't like all the bad feelings the conversation is stirring up inside me. I take a long drink of my beer.

"Did this Gertrude Stein tell you to go back to school?" I ask, my words as slurred as hers now.

"No, no, no, no ..." She opens her eyes and steadies herself against the bar. "I would never take *direction* from one of these experiences. I just receive what they impart. With Gertrude, I was filled with this feeling of possibility for my life and the idea that I wasn't thinking big enough. Maybe grad school was child's play. Maybe I should move to Paris or start hosting Saturday evening salons. Maybe I should take a lesbian lover. Maybe ... there was a much bigger life out there for me than an empty two-story house in a respectable suburb. Maybe my house was a metaphor for my life."

All the time she's talking I'm trying to be a good listener. I really am, but I'm just getting angrier and angrier, and I got no idea why. Then, all of a sudden, I start talking and I don't stop for nothing.

"You don't get to just choose your life like that," I say, getting louder and faster as I go, "You live somewhere in a group of people who think and act a certain way and you think and act just like 'em cuz you don't think to do otherwise or, if you *do* think about it, you gotta put it outta your head cuz, like you said, the urge to conform is a goddam strong force, and we're all stuck here in this world with its goddam boundaries and rules—and you don't hire people on your crews who don't look like you cuz, goddammit, nobody else does, and you sure as hell don't call out your uncle's bullshit even if the guy he won't hire is your friend cuz guys around here don't hire guys who don't look like 'em—and you're just trying to live your life, goddammit, make sure you got enough money to pay the bills, go out for a couple of beers on a Saturday night, keep your little girl safe, retire if you're lucky with a little nest egg, which you can do, goddammit, cuz you make forty-five a year, which I know, goddammit, is twice as much as a janitor makes at a factory in Burlington ... but you're part of a group and you gotta play by rules you didn't have no part in makin', and you don't get to choose, goddammit!" I slam back the rest of my beer and then slam my glass down on the bar.

"I don't believe that," Seraphina whispers, shaking her head, glassy-eyed. "And I don't think you do either."

"I do, goddammit, I do ..." I mutter into my empty glass.

She puts her arm around me, and goddammit, I start to cry. She pulls me closer. I put my head on her shoulder. Her hair smells so goddam good I can hardly stand it. We sway drunk on our bar stools for a while, and then she says, slurred and slow, "The good news, Rick ... is it's not too late."

"For what?" I ask, wishing I could keep my head on her shoulder forever.

She strokes my hair and answers real quiet, "For either of us."

That night, as I lay next to her in the hotel bed after she's asleep, my hand resting on the soft, warm curve of her hip, I try to sort through everything we talked about, try to figure out if she is, in fact, crazy. I can't come to any real conclusion on the matter, but, as I drift off to sleep, up on the ceiling, in the shadow cast by the streetlamp, I see the face of Trevon Williams.

DISCUSSION QUESTIONS

1 Why is Seraphina nervous to talk to the narrator? How does she characterize herself?

2 How did Seraphina feel when she "attended Pampered Chef parties, made small talk at school events, and drove a minivan?" How has her perspective changed in middle-age?

3 Why does Seraphina's daughter call her from Germany?

4 What is Seraphina's hypothesis about the urge to conform?

5 What does the narrator's daughter tell him about bias?

6 How does the narrator react to Seraphina sharing about her life? Based on his responses, do you like or dislike the narrator?

7 Why do you think the author chose the name Seraphina, as opposed to something simpler like "Sarah?"

8 Why do you think the narrator gets angry at the end of his conversation with Seraphina?

9 The narrator cries after Seraphina responds to his outburst–what might he be experiencing? What kind of change do you think the narrator goes through during his conversation with Seraphina?

10 How does Seraphina respond to the narrator's tirade? Why do you think Seraphina's actions affect the narrator so powerfully?

11 What parallels do you see between Seraphina and the narrator from "Bigfoot's Got a Lover?"

12 How would you compare Seraphina to the paranoid narrator of "When They Come for Me?"

13 What aspects of the story seem liminal to you? (Consider setting, characters, and action.) Is there a liminal guide, and if so, what is the nature of their interaction with other characters?

PRE-READING QUESTIONS

- If you were the parent of an eight-year-old child, would you try to protect her innocence or teach her about the real world?
- How does it make you feel that some kids have to grow up faster than their peers?

GOODBYE, BONAVENTO

PAPA USED TO HAVE A MONKEY. AN OLD CAPUCHIN NAMED Bonavento. He carries a picture in his coat pocket of them working together on the corner of Mulberry and Grand, taken by a newsman shortly after the Shamnais invaders began issuing historical street music licenses to Humans, long before I was born. In the picture, Papa is very handsome. He's wearing a straw boater and a red vest that doesn't have any stains or rips in it. His moustache curls up at the edges, and he still has all his teeth. I know because he's smiling in the picture, laughing as Human children dance barefoot around him. Bonavento, in his matching vest and tie, holds a tin cup out to the camera.

I came eight years ago. Born the same day Mama died. When I ask *how* she died, Papa just says, "Your mama was an angel who floated up to heaven," but I'm pretty sure he's making that part up. He also says, "It's a very good thing you came along when you did, my little Angela because I got used to having an angel around, and I don't know what I'd do without another one." I don't think he's making that part up.

It's been hard taking the place of an angel—sometimes I want to do naughty things like steal an apple from Mr. Garcia's cart when I am hungry or tell Mrs. Fischer to mind her own business when she scolds Papa for hanging our wash out the front window even though she knows we don't get any sun in the back—but it's been even harder taking the place of Bonavento. When Papa goes to work now, I hold the little tin cup out. I don't mind it. Mostly. But sometimes I wish I could go back to school. Papa says maybe next year, but I don't know. He worries what will happen to me if I'm away from him. And I worry what will happen to him if he's away from me.

Today we're on one of the Shamnais blocks. I tried to stop him from coming here. This morning, I said, "Papa, we should stay in the Human neighborhoods today."

But he replied, "No, no, my little angel, we cannot. There are too many organ grinders here now." Then he added sadly, "and they all have monkeys." I didn't say anything more. Mrs. Fischer has been yelling at him about the rent, and my breakfast this morning was the hard heel of the bread. Papa said he wasn't hungry, but he always says that when only the heel is left.

The wind is cold today and the sky gloomy. Papa says the invaders will want to dance to keep warm, but he has been cranking the organ for an hour now and not one of them has stopped. A group of older Shamnais boys passes by heckling him. Papa waves and smiles his toothless smile because they are smiling and laughing, and Papa doesn't understand what they say to him —what they call him outside the Human blocks. Sometimes, when he can tell from their faces or their gestures that what they're saying isn't kind, he asks me to translate, but I just tell him they want to hear a different song.

"Are you cold, Angela?" Papa stops cranking the barrel organ and frowns at my threadbare dress and jacket.

"No Papa," I reply but he can see that I am shivering.

"Maybe you could dance?" he suggests. "It will make you warmer."

"I'm fine," I say again and smile. I know he would like me to dance because then the Shamnais children might join in and their parents might give us a few coins, but I think he knows I'm too embarrassed, so he doesn't say anything more about it.

"I think we need to take our musical production uptown, little angel, where there is more interest in our ancient Human culture."

"I think this is a good spot," I say quietly. If we are to perform in the Shamnais neighborhoods, I prefer to stay in the poor ones, but I know that if we don't get any coins, there will be nothing to eat for supper.

"Maybe we will make something along the way," he says and turns the cart up the sidewalk, cranking it as we go. But it's hard for him to do both at once. The music comes out in fits and starts. Sometimes fast, sometimes slow. As we walk, I hold out the can, but I don't look up. Papa has the old kind of organ that plays the same six songs over and over. Not the new kind with the chips you can switch out for the new songs from the new shows.

I hear a coin clink in my can. It's a five-bit. I look up at Papa, surprised. He grins at me. "What do you say, my little angel, maybe a little oil tonight to eat with the bread?"

"Yes, Papa!" I smile at him and he grins even wider. I hold the can out toward a Shamnais female hurrying in our direction. He gives the barrel a vigorous crank, but she only glares at us as she passes. I pull the can back close against me and look down at my shoes.

We walk twelve blocks north. It's not really uptown. We just call it that. They have fancy houses up here with flower gardens and trees. The rich Shamnais girls wear pretty dresses, and the boys don't have holes in their pants. Everyone wears shoes. Papa wheels the organ to the side of a cafe and resumes his cranking. A coin clinks in my cup and soon after another! We smile at each other. I can almost smell the oil warming in the pan, taste it soaked into my bread. But the cafe owner comes out and starts yelling at Papa. The owner's face turns purple and spit flies out of his mouth as he points down the street and yells some more. Papa doesn't have to understand Shamnais to know what he is saying. He motions to me, and I follow him away from the cafe. Papa doesn't look at me. He doesn't crank the organ as we move.

"Papa," I say when I see the Washington Square Arch up ahead, "We can't perform in that park because of the ordinance, remember?"

"This park?" Papa asks, frowning. I don't know how he has forgotten. My heart pounds just looking at it. I don't know exactly what an ordinance is, but I know it's something bad because the mean old Shamnais who told us about it last time said we better go back to our own neighborhood or the city guard would come after us. Papa didn't know what he was saying, but I started crying, so Papa started yelling at him in Human, and then he started yelling at Papa in Shamnais, and then the fancy Shamnais from the fancy houses stopped and stared, and I whispered to Papa that the city guard was coming, and he put me on the cart and gave me a ride all the way back to Mulberry Street in the Human blocks.

Still frowning, Papa says, "But it's such a nice park with so many nice-looking invaders. I'm sure they will appreciate some nice music while they go for a stroll."

"Papa ..." I try again, but he doesn't hear because he is pushing the cart across the street and there is noise from the passing motorists. Halfway across, one of the cart wheels gets wedged in a pothole, and Papa cannot budge it. The motorists must make their way around us, some of them yelling at us in Shamnais. I worry the wheel will break and we will have no way of getting the organ back when we are this far from home, but a friendly Shamnais male dressed in fancy clothes stops to help us. He speaks to Papa in his own language while he helps, and Papa pretends to understand. I am relieved when they get the wheel out without breaking it.

"Thank you," Papa says, lifting his tattered straw boater.

I repeat it in Shamnais to make sure the man understands. He lifts his hat to Papa and smiles at me, making me blush. I follow Papa into the park. He wheels the organ just inside the arch and begins to turn the crank.

"Bonavento would bring in a fortune here," Papa says, nodding at all the clean, well-dressed Shamnais children and their clean, well-dressed parents. I'm sure he would have. On really good days, Bonavento would bring in half a month's rent, and we could buy vegetables and make soup and split a whole loaf of bread. He was so friendly and adorable, the Shamnais couldn't resist him. But, last year, he bit the face of one of their boys who grabbed him by the tail and swung him into a lamp post, and the city guard came and took him away. All night, Papa cried and muttered into his pillow in the corner where he sleeps on the floor. I pretended to be asleep but was frozen on my cot, staring up into the darkness, not knowing what to say or do and wondering how much Papa cried for Mama when she died. He only had Mama for three years, but he had Bonavento for eighteen. I wondered how much he'd cry for me.

A Shamnais male scowls and mutters in flawless Human, "For gods' sake, man," as he moves his family away from the music. Papa tries his best to keep the organ tuned but it is getting old, and the cold makes the high notes screech.

Clink, clink. An older Shamnais female drops in a few coins and gives me that look. I know it's a kind sort of look but, even so, it makes my face burn. I look down at my shoes.

A few of the Shamnais children begin to gather. Their parents hang back, talking with their friends. If Bonavento were here, he would go around tipping his hat to the males and kissing the hands of the females.

"You're nothing without a monkey," I heard another organ grinder say when word got around the Human neighborhoods that Bonavento had been taken away. After that, I kept asking Papa when we would buy another monkey, but he would always just say that we didn't really need one. Sometimes, though, I'd wake up in the night and see him counting coins from the rent can, and I wondered if he was telling the truth. I stopped asking him a couple of months ago.

A few more of the Shamnais children have gathered around to listen. But no one is dancing, and no one has given us any more coins. A big Shamnais boy shouts behind me and I drop the can. I'm a little jumpy in the Shamnais neighborhoods—nervous that someone will grab me and swing me into a lamp post. I bend over to pick up the coins before someone steals them. Papa gives the boy a stern look but keeps on cranking the organ.

"Are you all right, little angel?" he asks.

I nod and move away from the boy, then look past the children to their parents. I wish I had never come to understand what they whisper to each other about us. I wish I had never come to understand what their expressions mean. I wish, sometimes, that like Papa, I didn't understand their language. I could dance then and there would be more coins in our can and more soup for dinner and a new monkey to do tricks.

A new tune starts on the organ. The best one. A happy sounding tune that the children might dance to. One of the girls, my size in a blue dress with white ribbons, brings two small children to join the others around us.

"Where's your monkey?" she asks in Shamnais. I don't answer. Sometimes I pretend that I don't know their language when I don't want to answer. But sometimes I can't pretend. Sometimes I have to do the talking, translating back and forth, sometimes having to say things that Papa doesn't know about so I can keep him safe, like when they came to take away Bonavento. Papa was shouting at them, and one of the city guards started shouting back about a fine, and then about jail, but I interrupted and told them in my best Shamnais that Mama was dead and then, though I knew Papa wouldn't want me to say it, I told him we barely had money for food, and that's when the other guard gave me that look and told me that if we just put Bonavento in the cage for them, we wouldn't have to worry about any of the rest of it.

The happy tune is halfway over now. The next one is a little sad. The very old Humans like it but not the kids. The rich Shamnais parents will be too impatient to stay for it. The novelty of the organ grinders has worn off, and, unlike the poor Humans and Shamnais, they can afford access to all the wonderful music ever created by both species, and to go to the new shows and concerts. I should take the hand of one of their little ones and start dancing. If they dance, then the older children might too, and then I can take my can over to their parents who will feel obliged to put in a few coins, but when I think about dancing in front of them in their beautiful new clothes, my legs feel paralyzed.

Something across the park catches my eye. Two figures with funny hats. My heart begins to pound. The city guard. Papa sees them and frowns. He looks at me. In a few minutes they will be up here, and we will have to leave. He would like me to get the Shamnais children to dance so we can make a collection, but he won't ask. I know though that it is now or never.

Once before, I hesitated and missed my chance. It was when the city guards were about to take Bonavento away. The nice one came back into the apartment to ask me if I would like to come out into the hall to say goodbye. Papa was out there already sobbing and telling Bonavento how very sorry he was and what a good partner he had been and how he loved him and would never forget him, so loud that everyone in the whole apartment could hear. But my legs wouldn't move, so I just shook my head and stood there silent, my eyes fixed on my shoes while they took Bonavento away.

I glance at Papa. He tries not to look at me. He doesn't want to pressure me, but we both see that the guards are getting closer.

"Time to go," the Shamnais girl with the silky blue dress says in her own language to the little ones, so I force my legs to move. I hold out a hand to the little boy and he takes it, smiling. We start to dance. The little girl claps. I tuck the cup into the pocket of my jacket and take her hand as well.

I will have to time it just right—the dance, the collection, our exit out of the park—but I know I can't rush this part of it. Around and around, I spin the little Shamnais children, trying to remember to smile. Soon the rest of the children are dancing and laughing, and their parents are taking note. Papa is grinning just like in the picture in his pocket. Maybe we will have soup with our bread tonight. I curtsey to the little boy who giggles in front of me and take the can out of my pocket.

As I make my way over to their parents, Papa laughs happily and lifts his hat to them. Their eyes land on my approaching figure. I keep the smile on my face but squint to blur the expressions on theirs, and, as the jaunty notes of the old refrain repeat themselves, these words merge with them in my head—*Goodbye, Bonavento, Goodbye, Goodbye. Goodbye, Bonavento, Goodbye.*

❁

DISCUSSION QUESTIONS

1 Angela feels that "It's been hard taking the place of an angel." Why might she feel this way?

2 What does Angela say when her father asks if she's cold? Why do you think she says this?

3 Angela's father suggests that she could dance if she feels cold. How does Angela initially respond, and why? Why does she think her father wants her to dance?

4 What does Angela hear the Shamnais saying about her father? Why do you think she chooses not to translate for him? If you were her father, would you want her to translate or not? If you were Angela, would you choose to translate?

5 How does Angela's father respond when a Shamnais gives him directions in his own language? Why might he do this?

6 Why do you think the author chose to make the Shamnais a different species instead of rich people from Earth? How does this affect your feelings towards Angela and her father's predicament?

7 What does a Shamnais boy do to Bonavento, the monkey? What happens to Bonavento after that?

8 Why do you think Angela wonders how much her father would cry for her if she were taken away?

9 What does Angela wish she had never come to understand? Why do you think she wishes for this?

10 Why do you think Angela's face burns after a Shamnais drops coins in her bucket and gives her "a kind sort of look?"

11 Angela says that she knows her father "doesn't want to ask" her to dance, but she realizes he wants her to. Why might her father not want to ask her to dance? What does this tell you about his character?

12 Why does Angela dance even though she feels embarrassed? What does this tell you about her character?

13 Why do you think Angela has "to remember to smile" during the final dance with the Shamnais children? What does that tell you about how she feels in this moment?

14 Why do you think Angela is reminded of Bonavento as she dances with the Shamnais children? Why might she think specifically about saying goodbye to Bonavento in this moment?

15 Do you think the closing dance scene is happy or sad?

16 What aspects of the story seem liminal to you? (Consider setting, characters, and action.) Is there a liminal guide, and if so, what is the nature of their interaction with other characters?

PRE-READING QUESTIONS

- Have you ever given up on a dream? If so, why did you do it?
- If you had the choice of being famous for some great accomplishment or understanding the true nature of reality, which would you choose?
- If a mysterious cat showed up right now, would you follow it?

I FOLLOWED SCHRÖDINGER'S CAT AND HERE'S WHAT I FOUND

It never occurred to me that if Schrödinger's cat showed up, I shouldn't feed it, let alone follow it. A humble graduate student of philosophy without health insurance, boyfriend, or mentor, I'd been languishing in the department for years, processing an avalanche of data per my absentee advisor's direction without any advancement in my apperception.

I was the only one in our office that stifling hot day in September when she showed up. Sweating through my tank top and bored to dullness, I half-dozed under the ceiling fan, half-watched the Chinese lanterns twirl lazily from the ceiling in our otherwise drab and outdated office. I was just about to take another bite of a dry and mustardless turkey sandwich, wondering if maybe I should have purchased the tuna fish instead, when that dead-and-alive cat approached, silent and stealth, in her svelte tuxedo coat. I bolted upright in my chair. She purred and slunk around my legs, then leapt up onto one of the towering stacks of papers that lined the room. She traipsed across their tops until she reached the far side of the room and then sat down on a stack and stared at me. After considering each other for a bit, I made my way through the labyrinth of data I had yet to process and set my turkey sandwich down in front of her. But she only sniffed at it indifferently. Without even a nibble or the slightest indication of appreciation, she jumped down, paused at my advisor's brown corduroy jacket, which hung from the back of his chair, and rubbed her side against one of its worn, leather elbow patches. Then she made her way to a door I'd never noticed before and began to scratch at it. I went to the door, reached for the handle, and pulled it open. The cat ran through and, without hesitation, I followed.

You may be thinking this was foolish. That I should have gotten someone to go with me or at least have arranged to have a spotter at the entrance. But I was never celebrated for my street smarts, and the urge to see what was beyond the door overwhelmed me.

My eyes couldn't make out anything at first, but my ears were confronted with a clamorous clickety-clacking. Despite the racket, I could hear the door beginning to creak shut behind me. I whirled around, trying to catch it before it closed, but was too late and could only watch with near simultaneous waves of alarm, regret, and relief, as the door closed and dissolved into the wall.

The cat meowed. At least curiosity hadn't killed her—if you could even kill a cat both dead and alive. I turned to see where she had gone and found that I'd entered some sort of boundless space, well-lit and ordered with rows and rows of Borel's infinite monkeys sitting, as you might reasonably expect, at their desks, poking away at the keys of their typewriters.

You might be surprised, though, to find out that, contrary to our collective imaginings, Borel's infinite monkeys are not chimpanzees—which, I politely remind you, are *apes*—but, rather, proboscis monkeys with their peerless and peculiarly preeminent noses. You will, I think, be amused to hear that, when I squinted, these monkeys, with their baldish heads and mutton chops, appeared as mashups of the lettered gentlemen of the late nineteenth century and hirsute Cyrano de Bergeracs composing their masterpieces for posterity.

From somewhere down one of the rows the cat meowed. I worried a little that her getting lost amongst the monkeys would catalyze some sort of dimensional fusion that would crash the spacetime matrix, but I had more pressing concerns. Borel had taught us that somewhere out there one of these monkeys had almost surely typed the *Complete Works of William Shakespeare*, and I was on a mission to find it. Not since Sir Galahad sallied forth to find the Holy Grail had any seeker set about a quest with such desire and determination.

That was at the beginning of course. I didn't understand at the time that all such quests led seekers through some sort of wasteland—mine, a midcentury modern monoscheme of monkeys multiplying meaninglessness. After a while I simply found myself lost without a sense of time or place. As I trudged down the endless rows, peering over the shoulders of the proboscises peppering their papers with cumulations of characters, I began to wonder what exactly I was doing. Why I had come. What sort of fool undertook this sort of journey. Dulled into a daze by the tintinnabulation of the typewriters, I eventually began to forget why I was there.

Then, one day, I was startled from my stupor. For there, in the middle of a long paragraph of H's and 3's, appeared that most famous of Shakespeare's lines: "To be, or not to be, that is the question." Blinking and dumb with astonishment, I stopped in my tracks and stared at those ten words whose presence laid bare the width and the depth and the height and the breadth of the infinitude through which I wandered.

I fell to my knees. I wept the purest of tears from the purest of hearts. Joy and wonder were mine! But, sadly, for only a few moments. It wasn't long before secondary considerations crept in. This discovery—*my discovery*—was monumental. A career-maker. A stupid grin spread across my face. My eyes grew wide at the thought of publicity appearances, lecture circuits, and interviews with Oprah.

But what if I *stayed*? If I kept looking, I would almost surely find the entire manuscript of *Hamlet*. Or *Macbeth*! And if I *never* stopped—if I kept looking forever and ever—I would almost surely find the *Complete Works of William Shakespeare*, possibly even annotated. Then, well, there would be *no* going back. But if I returned with at least this one sentence—perfectly wrought in the dimensional quadrille of spacetime, randomly repeated in the singular totality that is infinitude—people would cry, "*Miracle!*" And they wouldn't be wrong because such occurrences, though possible within the scope of the infinite, are extraordinary when experienced in spacetime. But if I stayed to chase down even the rest of Hamlet's famous soliloquy, it would mean giving up everything I had ever known.

It's fair if you're thinking that it would be no great loss. I understand that I'm no Hypatia of Alexandria or Simone de Beauvoir but, even so, I am a person. With a life. Maybe not much of one, but even if I had health insurance with no deductible *or* co-pays, a handsome *and* intelligent fiancé who *loved* me, *and* a world-famous advisor who actually *cared* about my academic career, to return and seek such affirmation and adulation after the appearance of that insubordinate iambic pentameter seemed—yes, I will use the word even though it may result in the rejection of my account of these events by all respectable publications and personages—a *sin*. But here is where I must make my confession. In the end, my concern for credentials overrode everything else. I lunged toward the desk and ripped the paper from the typewriter.

The monkey honked long and loud. The cavernous nostrils of his curious nose flared. I apprised him of the urgent business requiring his presence in spacetime, but he just honked all the louder. When I tried to pull him from his chair, he began to scream, which caused all the other monkeys in the vicinity to begin to scream as well. It wasn't until I promised to get him a new typewriter if he went back with me that he quieted down, got off his chair, and took my hand. At that point, the rest of the dactylographic monkeys resumed their typing in perfect synchronicity, and I called for the cat.

"Here, kitty, kitty ..." Instantly, the door reappeared in front of me, and a cat meowed behind me. I turned to watch as she ambled disinterestedly in my direction. When I turned back to the door, I wasn't so much surprised as fascinated by the interdisciplinary cooperation to find Maxwell's demon blocking it. There he sat in a tacky red devil costume with pointy ears and a tail, his legs crossed and one arm flung over the back of a chair, an impish grin on his face. The cat sprawled out underneath the chair and began to lick her underside.

"Well, well, well," the demon said, "what do we have here?"

"Wouldn't you like to know?" I retorted. I was somewhat familiar with this demon from an undergraduate physics course.

I knew he wanted information, but I wasn't about to reveal anything until I knew what he was up to.

"I see you've brought a friend," he smirked, nodding at the monkey. "Borel won't be happy."

"Isn't infinity minus one still infinity?"

"Sassy!" the demon laughed, though it wasn't exactly sinister like you might expect—more like devilish amusement. Suddenly, he seemed really familiar.

"What's your name?" I asked.

He scowled, "Maxwell never bothered to give me one."

"I mean, do I *know* you?" I pressed, leaning in closer and squinting at him.

"I'll answer your question if you answer mine," he replied.

I crossed my arms and waited, a skeptical eyebrow raised.

"Besides this monkey, which I may or may not allow, what is it you want to bring back with you into the one-through-four?" he asked.

"Well," I replied, clearing my throat and straightening out the paper, which had become wrinkled and sweaty in my determined grip, "*This*." I held it out for him to read.

The demon pulled a pair of readers out of the breast pocket of his costume and put them on. He looked at the page for a bit before his face brightened with delight.

"Ah ... a riddle!" he shouted gleefully. "The game is afoot!" He got up then and did a little dance. Alarmed, the cat ran off down the rows of monkeys, who honked and screamed for a few seconds, then stopped in synchronicity and resumed their typing.

"Look, I'm not interested in riddles," I explained, "I just want to get back to the other side to share what I've found."

The demon stopped dancing and looked at me. "Really? That's your priority?"

My face grew as red as his costume.

"Well, sure ..." I fumbled. The monkey honked and tugged on my hand. "And to get this guy a new typewriter."

"You would willingly go back to the Chinese Room after

seeing what you've seen?" Now it was the demon's turn to cross his arms and raise a skeptical eyebrow.

"To share my discovery with others..." I replied unconvincingly. "And besides," I said with a sniff, "I believe you have the wrong idea about my work back in spacetime—my work in the Chinese Room was simply an *experiment*."

"Was it?" the demon asked coyly.

"Yes, it was. Assigned to me by my advisor."

"And who exactly *is* your advisor?" The demon leaned in closer. His eyes danced and his mouth smirked. I leaned in as well and squinted into his very familiar face.

"You!" I cried.

At this, the demon convulsed with laughter and shouted, "I moonlight as a philosophy professor!" Then he broke out into another impish dance. I crossed my arms and glared at him.

When he was finally finished, I asked through gritted teeth, "Is the costume really necessary?"

"Of course not. But it makes it all so much more interesting, don't you think?" He gave a dramatic flourish of his tail. The monkey honked and let go of my hand, then went and sat down on the chair and sighed.

"Look," I said, "I don't know what this is all about. All I know, is I have something in my possession that can help the human mind grasp the scope of infinity—the nature of eternity."

Again, the demon-slash-advisor stopped dancing and looked at me. "You think anyone trapped in that room can comprehend this? That they'll *believe* you?"

"Hopefully, there's no more than a handful of schmucks like me out there trapped by their *advisor* in the Chinese Room," I replied bitterly.

"Well, that's where you've got it all wrong," he said with another dramatic flourishing of his fake tail. "That room isn't just for graduate students and thought experiments—that room is the *whole world*. Most people won't even accept what you have to say. It's too much to absorb, too vast to comprehend, too laden with implication. It's easier," he concluded smugly, as he examined the pointy tip of his tail, "to stay in the room."

"Even so ..." I began but was interrupted by the demon, who began stomping his feet and shouting.

"You have touched the infinite and *still* you want to go back? And don't try to tell me again it's for the greater good of humanity!"

I looked sheepishly at the monkey, now sitting with his legs crossed and his arm thrown over the back of the chair, but he just sighed again and looked away. The demon continued with exaggerated, condescending patience.

"To be or not to be, that *is* the question, but not the way it's meant in the one-through-four where death is of ultimate concern. I mean the way it's meant here in the zeroth dimension where your being resides in the *infinite now*—'eternity' some might call it. Sure, sure, there are disputes and dissections regarding the interchangeability of the terms, but we can at least all agree it's impossible for the human mind to grasp the full picture and that your limited conceptualizations are further complicated by the rather consequential limitations of your language—but I tell you, if you return with your current intentions to that quartet of dimensions oft referred to as 'spacetime,' you will relinquish the immediacy of your contact with the infinite. It will become a mere memory of an experience—documented, explained, defended, debated, doubted, and mocked, eventually reduced to a Wikipedia entry as the Borel's Infinite Monkey Hoax, *or* ..." but here he had to pause because the prodigy proboscis honked and flailed his arms in protest, only calming down when I assured him I would never let that last part happen. When he was quiet again, I turned back to the demon.

"Or *what*?" I asked.

"You can stay here and explore."

"Which means ... no Nobel Prizes ..."

"Or internet trolls or detractors."

"No press or publications ..."

"Or endless debates and defenses,"

I looked back at the rows of monkeys pecking away at their keys. Somewhere out there one of them was almost surely typing the script for *King Lear* and was about to start on *Romeo and Juliet*. Chastened, I handed the monkey his paper and patted him on the shoulder. He honked gratefully, then left in search of his typewriter.

"Do we need to find the cat or anything ..." I asked, "before I get lost in here again?"

"Nah," he replied, "When she gets hungry, she'll pop back into the one-through-four." He moved the chair aside. "Just remember to call for her if you want to pop back in yourself."

"What?" I stammered, "I thought ..."

"You thought, you thought, you thought!" he cried, raising his hands to the sides of his head but restraining himself from another temper tantrum. "Half the time it's the *not thinking* that's the trouble and the other half it's the *thinking* that's the trouble! Listen, you can come back in as much as you want now because you'll be bringing usable energy into the one-through-four. As long as you don't get your priorities messed up, that is, and start increasing the entropy over there, you've got a free pass."

"An interdimensional free pass ..." I mused, "this is better than a Ph.D."

"Well, don't get too excited. You're restricted to the zero-through-four for now, but, once you've found the collected works of the illustrious Willy Shakes, well, let's just say the multiverse is your playground."

"Wait ... so ... there *is* a multiverse?"

The demon rolled his eyes, sighed, and explained with exasperation, "It's not like I can go exploring for other universes or anything while I'm stuck here managing this door, but the possibilities *are* infinite so ..." He shrugged noncommittally, then called for the cat. She reappeared within moments, approaching as though on a leisurely stroll, then went and scratched at the door. The demon opened it, and together they passed back into spacetime.

As the door creaked shut, I watched my advisor pull back the hood of his demon costume and slip into the brown corduroy jacket with the worn leather elbow patches, preparing, I supposed, to lure other unwitting humans into his scheme of existential entropy reduction. Just before the door closed and dissolved into the wall, I saw him toss Schrödinger's cat the rest of my turkey sandwich, but she only sniffed at it indifferently.

I turned around and looked at the monkeys, the cacophony of their clacking keys and carriage returns now the sweet sounds of a symphony to me. One of them somewhere was almost surely typing the *Complete Works of William Shakespeare*, and I had eternity to find it.

❁

DISCUSSION QUESTIONS

1 Why does the narrator compare herself to Sir Galahad?

2 After the narrator's initial excitement wears off, how does her experience change? What might this description be trying to tell us about the process that faces all "seekers?"

3 There are a lot of metaphors for seeking knowledge: the author could have depicted the narrator searching for such things as a source of light, a fountain of wisdom, or a mirror of nature. Instead, the author draws on Borel's infinite monkey theorem, which states, "A monkey hitting keys at random on a typewriter keyboard for an infinite amount of time will almost surely type any given text, including the complete works of William Shakespeare." What might this particular choice of metaphor communicate to us about the author's view of discovery?

4 How does the narrator feel after she discovers a line from Hamlet?

5 Why do you think the author chose to have the narrator discover "To be or not to be–that is the question" as opposed to another famous line from Shakespeare? In what way is this a story about choice, questions, or the nature of existence?

6 What does the narrator imagine doing with her discovery?

7 What argument does the narrator's dissertation advisor, dressed as Maxwell's demon, make to her when she's considering going back?

8 Maxwell's demon is a thought experiment imagining a hypothetical creature who can sort molecules of gas based on their speed. (If this demon could effortlessly separate low and high energy particles, the energy preserved would challenge the traditional understanding of thermodynamic entropy). How might the dissertation advisor's advice to the narrator relate to the idea of entropy–the gradual decline into disorder–or perhaps function as a challenge to the law of entropy?

9 What do you think is the right choice for the protagonist: explore the infinite forever, looking for the complete works of William Shakespeare or go back to spacetime? Which would you do? Is your answer similar to the one you gave before you read the story?

10 Does the end of the story strike you as optimistic or pessimistic? Why?

11 What aspects of the story seem liminal to you? (Consider setting, characters, and action.) Is there a liminal guide, and if so, what is the nature of their interaction with other characters?

PRE-READING QUESTIONS

- Do you remember where you were when you first realized other people had their own lives apart from you? How old were you? What was the experience like?
- Have you ever had times when you thought of your parents that way? Not just as you parents, but as people with their own experiences and feelings? What happened?

THE UNEXPECTED CONSEQUENCE OF AN UNSOLICITED REVOLUTION

When Evy was small she thought she was the center of it all. Faces flitted in and out of view like planets around their little sun. Mother. Father. Neighbor. Friend. The milkman with his clinking bottles. The mailman with his bag. Apart from her, their lives were naught. Outside her home, it held true too—the German shepherd growling in the alley existed only as a terrifying obstacle to a friend's house, and the preschool teacher reading stories to children fanned out around her feet existed only in the little schoolhouse a few blocks down the street.

At some point in those earliest years Evy became aware of her *self*, that little star burning bright at the center of things. Walking in a pretty dress into the living room she thought to herself, *I am walking in this pretty dress.* Talking to her friend about a bird's nest they found, she thought to herself, *I am talking to my friend about this bird's nest.* This self-realization only further established her position—firmly fixed her already shining place in the heavens —and Evy continued on about her days playing in *her* neighborhood and living in *her* house, where the refrigerator held the food *she* ate and the bookshelves held the books *she* read and her mother kissed her forehead and made her cookies as she orbited around Evy, the little sun.

One late summer afternoon, when Evy was seven, she looked out across the parking lot of the city pool while unlocking her bike after a day of swimming. Her warm, wet bathing suit clung uncomfortably beneath her sundress and the smell of chlorine emanated from her skin as her gaze fell upon the sweat-soaked back of a woman digging for something in the middle seat of a rusted, purple van.

Behind Evy the squeals of children splashing in the water rose and fell and, beneath her, waves of heat rippled up off the pavement, pushing upward, stretching the white-blue sky to the point of bursting, but her attention zeroed in past the long row of station wagons and boxy sedans to the middle seat of that van. Evy tilted her head to the side and squinted as a new thought blossomed gently in her mind: This woman was looking in *her* purse, viewing things through *her* eyes and feeling them in *her* hands—the weighty metal of a set of keys, the smooth plastic of a sunscreen bottle, the loose, pinching hinge of her sunglasses. She might be tired or frustrated or eager to get inside. She might be early. She might be late. She might be exactly on time, but she was there in that parking lot, picking up her kids from that pool, and, from *that* woman's vantage point, all the people around her, *including Evy*, were just little planets in a world that revolved around *her*.

Evy looked up and around then, mouth parted and eyes darting inside her motionless head, as she took in her surroundings through this new lens. A skinny boy jumped off a nearby park bench. A wrinkled woman walked her poodle. Two shirtless teenage boys tore out of the parking lot in their pickup truck blasting KISS.

All of them suns in their own worlds.

All their worlds overlapping.

A Copernican revolution of the mind but, at the age of seven, Evy didn't know what to do with it. She just stood there next to her banana seat bike, in awe of the revelation meted out to her on a cracked patch of asphalt outside the city pool. Half a minute later her stomach rumbled its ravenous post-swimming growl and she hopped on her bike and rode for home, fixated on the Hostess CupCakes stashed in her closet, forgetting, until she lay fed and exhausted on her bed that night, about the other four billion suns floating around on planet Earth.

As with all revolutions, consequences followed.

The curious insight that day at the pool merged with an empathetic nature further sensitized when a black hole passed near enough her celestial position to yank a body of great significance out from orbit around the little sun and fling it far into the recesses of the universe. The smiling face that read her stories and bandaged her knees was, one day, no longer there. The priest said the Lord took her, but her father said it was cancer. Either way, her mother was gone. Evy made no explicit connection between any of this—she was only in the second grade—but, nevertheless, it began to affect her.

In elementary school, Evy would be playing bionic woman at recess and notice the girl with the greasy hair and the uneven gait standing alone and staring out through her coke bottle glasses at the other children laughing and playing, and Evy would be stopped in her secret agent tracks by a terrible sadness. In middle school, she would be racing to finish her conjugation worksheet before her academic nemesis finished hers but then would catch a glimpse of the boy who drew amazing insect monsters and who would cry at least once a week bury his face in his hands, and the terrible sadness would take hold of her. Evy's rival would run her paper up to Sister Mary Therese, but Evy would remain at her desk, rapt and trembling, feeling the boy's agony as he packed up his things for the day, feeling his shame and confusion as he walked down the long, dark corridor in dread of yet another phone call home.

Then there was the summer before her junior year. On a sweltering evening at the county fair while making out with her boyfriend behind the grandstand as Cheap Trick crooned to half-filled bleachers, she caught sight of a carnie at the distant, grassy edge of the fairgrounds, sitting alone on a stool behind his trailer, staring down at the ground. She didn't even notice when the blond, bronzed boy slipped his hand up under her shirt because the terrible sadness fell like a pall over the fairgrounds and all she could think about was what the man behind the trailer was thinking about. *His mother? His brother? A girl he once loved? The circumstances that led up to that moment? To his sitting there on that stool behind that trailer at that county fair filled with beefy farm kids and mulleted teenagers?*

After that, barely a day went by that she didn't see the terrible sadness lurking somewhere, dogging some unfortunate soul, and it all culminated one late spring evening about a month before her high school graduation. Evy was sitting at a table on the first floor of the public library, chewing on a pencil eraser and listening to Pink Floyd on her Walkman. She'd been there for several hours already, supposedly studying for a history exam with her best friend Theobald, but they'd spent the whole time sneaking Pop Rocks and arguing in impassioned whispers about the existence of God and the meaning of various lyrics on *The Wall*. Theo was gone now but Troy, who had just finished a parent-mandated tutoring session, was throwing notes at her from the table behind, and she kept replying because, well, she was single at the moment and it was always fun to flirt with a guy who looked like Matt Dillon, even if she had a ton of work to do and the rest of the week was packed with two shifts at the corner market, a tennis meet, a choir concert, and a deadline for laying out the final issue of the school newspaper. Maybe she should have stayed home to study—it would have been less distracting. But then again, certain types of quiet were distracting, too, and much less pleasant than philosophical banter with your best friend and flirty exchanges with the high school hottie.

Another note flicked against the back of her head. Evy picked it up and smoothed it out on the table. "CREEK?" it asked in perfect block letters, followed by a winky face. Evy smiled, eyebrows raised. Troy always carried a blanket and a six-pack in the trunk of his muscle car, and she knew from other girls in her class how an evening at the creek with him usually ended up. An attractive offer, but, as a young woman coming of age in the late eighties, her twelve years of Catholic education all seemed to boil down to the single, searing commandment: *Thou shalt not have premarital sex*. And so Evy—in fellowship with all the martyrs and saints who had gone before her and persevered in virtue under equally trying circumstances—scrawled "MUST STUDY!!!" She drew a smiley face on the note and then tossed it over her shoulder onto Troy's table.

He left shortly after, winking at her as he passed, and Evy looked down at her work with a satisfied smile. It was always nice to know someone like Troy wanted you even if you'd never meet up with him at the creek. She opened *Crime and Punishment* to reread the last few pages of the epilogue, then reviewed the last paragraph she had written. At last ready to dive in, Evy took a quick glance up at the clock to see how many minutes she had left before the librarian kicked her and the other stragglers out. But as her eyes made that three-quarter-inch adjustment back down to her thesis, she caught sight of a middle-aged Korean man slouching at the last table between the A-frame of pulp fiction and the wobbly, revolving rack of books on tape. A ballpoint pen poked up out of the front pocket of his faded, beige button-up shirt, and a pair of worn khakis terminated at his scuffed brown shoes in the shadows beneath the table. A crop of shiny, short, black hair retreated from a high, smooth forehead, and the bridge of his nose wrinkled between squinting, brown eyes, as his thin lips pressed together in thought. But these details faded away as the preoccupation inhabiting his countenance took the foreground, throwing into relief an unnamed sorrow that laid squatter's claim deep in the lines of his weary face.

Evy braced herself.

She looked down at her notes, a scribbled mass of hieroglyphs in the margins. She tried to read, but all she could make out was the giant "X" she had made through the second half of the page. She needed to study, but it was of no account.

She was trying to make valedictorian, but it didn't matter. She had frittered away two hours of library time and now only forty-five minutes remained, *but it came anyway*. Like an asteroid hurtling through the blackness, obliterating everything in its way, the terrible sadness slammed her from her perch in the heavens into orbit around the slouching man's sun.

Evy gripped the table edge, her fingers numb from the pressure, her jaw clenched as the man's eyes glazed over. But her efforts were futile. The tsunami of his grief and regret and confusion came crashing in on her. She looked away. Tried to think of Pop Rocks and Pink Floyd and muscle cars and creek banks, but the terrible sadness rushed around her and pushed up passed her knees. It lapped threateningly at the tabletop, then surged up over it, consuming her notes. Steadily it rose, pushing against her chest, making it harder to breathe. Soon she would be unable to breathe at all.

Evy looked toward the slouching man, but he was gone. Even so, his sorrow rose unabated. It pressed upward past her chin. She lifted her face and strained on her toes, gulping panicked breaths above the froth.

Her eyes, just inches now above the raging whirlpool, darted in all directions. She craned her neck, searching for the man as it swelled above her lips, swallowed up her nose and eyes, pushing upward and upward until she was submerged. Her gently sprayed spikes of hair held out for a moment, then gave way as well, swishing resignedly above her in the flood.

There—on the third-floor rotunda where the state blue books and microfiche collected dust, the image of the man in beige rippled. He leaned forward over the balustrade.

But what was he doing up there? With his glassy look and that unnamed sorrow deep in the lines of his face? Was he about to do something ... final? She should go to him ... but she couldn't. *She didn't know him. It was none of her business. He might yell at her. Other people might hear. She had deadlines to meet. Responsibilities to tend to. A father who needed her. A curfew that soon expired.*

The fountains of the abyss burst forth and the flood gates of the firmament opened wide, burying her in the deepest and most desperate of seas.

He might be crazy. She shouldn't talk to strangers. There were professionals who dealt with this kind of thing. Medications to take the edge off.

But *she* was there. *Now*. How hard was it to push back her chair and stand up? To lift her foot and place it out front. To bring the other up and do the same. To walk across the room. Ascend the stairs. Extend a simple word. In case ... just in case ... he was about to succumb.

Then, she was pushing back her chair and rising to her feet. A great sucking noise ripped through the rolling depths like someone had pulled the plug from a giant tub. The terrible sadness whirled and began to drain. Evy lifted her face above the whirlpool. She pushed her left foot forward and then her right, propelling her way through his sorrow with her arms. Soon she was wading, then slogging across the soggy carpeting, ascending the stairs.

The man leaned forward heavily. His hands spread wide on the balustrade, his regret and heartache, unbearable weights hanging round his neck.

Just a few yards more.

What was that in his hand pressed against the rail? A book?

Yes.

She could start there.

Just ask him about the book.

A simple question and a smile.

A way to begin.

Her fingertips fluttered across the pocked old lacquer of the balustrade. Tingled as she neared. Even just the thought of the words spilling from her lips bringing the rushing promise of respite.

The man turned his face toward her, his glassy eyes registering confusion and then a spark of something that encouraged her a step closer. Evy stopped a bit before him, rested her trembling hand on the balustrade and opened her mouth to speak.

❁

DISCUSSION QUESTIONS

1 What does the metaphor of a "little sun" suggest about how Evy views herself as a child?

2 What does Evy realize when she's seven years old and sees a woman looking for something in a rusted, purple van? What does she then consider when she sees a skinny boy, a wrinkled woman walking her poodle, and teenage boys in a pickup truck?

3 What does the metaphor "A Copernican revolution of the mind" tell you about Evy's experience?

4 What distracts Evy while she's making out with her boyfriend under the bleachers? What does this tell you about what Evy is like? What about Evy's personality or life experience might make her likely to react in this way?

5 Evy is reading a Dostoevsky novel about a man who feels crushing guilt after murdering an elderly woman. Given that Evy is not contemplating murder, how might Evy's choice of novel reflect her experience and interests?

6 The narrator describes Evy's experience of feeling "a terrible sadness" "like an asteroid hurtling through the blackness." What provokes this sadness? What does the metaphor of the asteroid suggest about how Evy feels in this moment?

7 What does Evy try to talk herself out of doing after she sees the man at the balustrade? What reasons does she give?

8 What does Evy decide to do? Why do you think she is able to do this? What about Evy makes her more equipped to do this than the other students at the library?

9 What aspects of the story seem liminal to you? (Consider setting, characters, and action.) Is there a liminal guide, and if so, what is the nature of their interaction with other characters?

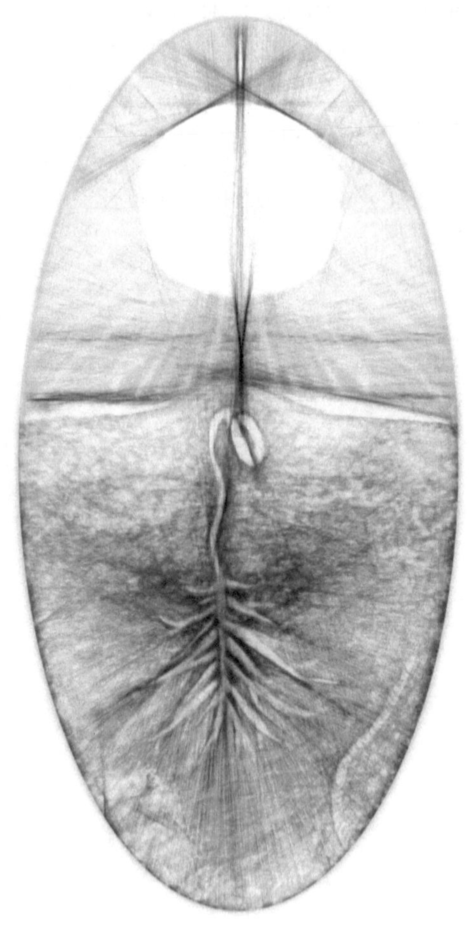

PRE-READING QUESTIONS

- What would you describe as the most difficult season of your life? What made it so challenging?

SUMMONED BY A STAR

YOUR LIFE BEGINS AS A SEED ATOP A STALK, BENEATH azure skies, in golden hues of wheat and sun. You sway in the summer breeze on rolling hills of grain until one day you're mowed down, plunged into the earth, cut off from the light. You tremble in the darkness.

Cool drops trickle down to you. Nourished, you send forth a tiny shoot, knowing you weren't meant for this everlasting night. Mole tunnels through. Worm and Beetle wriggle by. You summon life from your nascent store and a strange new growth anchors you. You send your shoot higher but still there is only darkness. Beetle waddles again across your path, searching for her own. Worm inches past, blindly eating his way forward. You try to settle into shadow, but you ache for the light.

Time passes. The earth cracks. Your thirst claws. Your pretty, silken skirt of roots lies limp. You send what you can to your shoot, but it isn't enough. If you had tears you would weep. Beetle is too free. She munches near your roots, stomping, oblivious, on their fragile tips. You drift into memories of golden light and gentle rain, the sound of wind and cicadas. But you no longer believe in your vision. Bitterness wracks your desiccated body. Your striving dries up, like the earth that has entombed you.

Then, a great rumbling convulses you. You've felt it before, one raging night of violent light before you came to this. But no—that was just a dream. The earth booms again. The shock reverberates through your delicate spine. One more and you'll be shattered. Pieces for Beetle to munch. But then you feel something. A drop of water slides down your shoot and lands on your withered roots. Then another. And another. Soon mud oozes around your roots, and you drink, drink, drink, until you are sated. Life wells up inside you!

But the mud begins to surge. Water rushes through Mole's tunnel, heaving up your roots. You try to hold on but you flounder. Beetle scurries for shelter beneath your skirt. You heave and sway, then the mud gives way, and she spins away on her back. You extend a tendril, but she cannot take hold. Her tiny legs claw above her, as she slips away into Mole's tunnel. The current pulls but you resist, though only a moment ago you were resigned to die. Worm thrashes toward you in desperate course. You lean into the deluge. Make a bridge with your body. He inches over you and continues upward. The water whirls. Your tender shoot flails in the torrent. Then everything grows still and soundless, and you lie listless in the mud.

Slowly, the water recedes. Beetle lies motionless on her back. You hope Worm has made it out. You try again to accept your lot, but something tugs at you from above. Primordial possibilities tingle. The force of it snaps you aright. Emboldened, you bore deeper with your roots, then reach and stretch to a point beyond bearing, until at last, summoned by a star, you break through to the surface, and the brilliance of the sunlit field is once again yours.

❁

DISCUSSION QUESTIONS

1 "Summoned by a Star" is written in the second person ("You sway in the breeze" as opposed to "I sway in the breeze," or "A flower sways in the breeze.") What effect does reading a story about "you" instead of "a flower" have on your experience of reading?

2. How does the seedling in this story feel while it is underground? Why does it feel this way?
3. Why do you think the plant in the story knows it is not meant for "everlasting night"? How does this compare to your own mindset when dealing with difficult times in your life?
4. Why do you think the author chose to set most of "Summoned by a Star" underground?
5. What attitude does the seedling have towards the beetle and worm as they pass by? Why do you think the author chose these interactions instead of, say, having the plant interact with a gardener? Do the seedling's attempts to help the beetle and worm drain its energy or contribute to its eventual breakthrough?
6. The author says that the seedling is "summoned by a star" as opposed to saying that it tries to find sunshine. What might the idea of being "summoned" to something as opposed to simply trying to find something on your own suggest about how a person might make it through a difficult time?
7. What aspects of the story seem liminal to you? (Consider setting, characters, and action.) Is there a liminal guide, and if so, what is the nature of their interaction with other characters?

ACKNOWLEDGEMENTS

Thank you to Dr. Timothy Carson for his contributions to the *Tales From the Liminal Study Edition* and the permission to use An Introduction to Liminality from *Leaning into the Liminal: A Guide for Counselors and Companions*; and to Dr. Matthew Flaherty for the thought-provoking pre-reading and discussion questions.

Timothy Carson is a writer, teacher, TedX speaker, and web curator. He is the author and editor of numerous books on liminality and teaches liminal studies in the Honors College of the University of Missouri.

Matthew Flaherty is an Irish-American poet and teacher with a passion for helping readers find beauty and humor in life's unforgettable moments. He has a PhD in British Literature and lives in Baltimore with his wife and two boys.

Sandra Kaye Kruse always wanted to be an author. After a stunning debut in *The Onion*, however, she found herself on a twenty-five-year sabbatical to raise eleven children. Since emerging from this truth-is-stranger-than-fiction period of her life, her writing has been longlisted for the John Steinbeck Award for Fiction and has won multiple awards in the National League of American Pen Women's "Soul-Making Keats Literary Competition."

skkruse.com

www.ingramcontent.com/pod-product-compliance
Lightning Source LLC
LaVergne TN
LVHW051006080826
845145LV00009B/2484

* 9 7 8 1 9 4 4 5 2 1 3 6 3 *